# ONGHORN COUNTRY

He     s a man of two tribes and his
C(     che blood was that of one of the
m      rage raiders of the south-west, but a
w.     an had raised him and there was as
mu     iate as duty mixed in with those
yea    They called him Blaine, a name
knc    across Texas: a man who was willing
to     judged by his actions. He was
esse   lly a loner with a void in his heart
that   ld never be filled, unless he killed
the n  n who had raised him – a man to
whom he owed everything. And Blaine
always paid his debts.

# LONGHORN COUNTRY

*by*

Tyler Hatch

**Dales Large Print Books**
Long Preston, North Yorkshire,
BD23 4ND, England.

British Library Cataloguing in Publication Data.

Hatch, Tyler
      Longhorn country.

A catalogue record of this book is
available from the British Library

ISBN   1-84262-490-3 pbk
ISBN   978-1-84262-490-6 pbk

First published in Great Britain in 2005 by Robert Hale Limited

Published in Large Print 2006 by arrangement with
Robert Hale Ltd.

Dales Large Print is an imprint of Library Magna Books Ltd.

Printed and bound in Great Britain by
T.J. (International) Ltd., Cornwall, PL28 8RW

# PROLOGUE

## END OF SEARCH

He hadn't slept deeply or soundly for the last five years so he heard the horsemen riding into the ranchyard long before someone threw a handful of gravel against his window pane. He slid the window up in its frame and moonlight glinted on his cap of thick silver hair as he leaned out, shotgun in hand, plain for all of the dozen horsemen below to see.

'It better be good!'

'Best news we've had in a coon's age, Morg!' called back the leader, standing beside his sweat-polished mount. 'Scout rode in with a stone arrer-head in his ass – got it runnin' away from a bunch of Comanche.' The man paused and added with an edge of excitement. 'Bunch led by an Injun with a yaller band of feathers in his headdress.'

Morgan O'Day's grip tightened on the shotgun and he felt as if all the air had been punched from his lungs.

It took him long seconds to find enough breath to ask, 'Yellow Wolf?'

'It's him, Morg – and he's got his whole kit-an'-kaboodle with him, pitchin' camp up in the Saltlicks, squaws, kids, the lot. And the scout's pretty sure she's with him!'

Morgan still couldn't breathe. *Five long years he'd searched for Katy! Hell, he'd hungered for her a lot longer than that – fifteen years easy– But she'd married Adam Blaine, dead long since, then been kidnapped by this bastard calling himself Yellow Wolf... And now at long last, she was back where he could reach her, rescue her from the hell she must have been through.*

'Be right down, Marsh!' Morgan O'Day managed to croak at last. 'Get the boys from the bunkhouse. Tell 'em to bring plenty of ammo!'

The Indians figured they were safe in the Saltlicks. They always had been, and Comanche were prone to routine: camp for the summer in one place, head out in the fall for better protection from the snow and cold before winter set in, come on down from the hills to make for the same spring campsite – round and round, following a gigantic circle that took in country in three, sometimes four, States.

Creatures of habit – and it was to be their undoing. Usually, they had always been well-settled in the Saltlicks camps, heavily guarded and protected, before the white men knew they were back. But this time was different – the wounded scout had brought invaluable news to Morg O'Day and the other ranchers and townsmen who had lost family to the Comanche in that devastating raid five years ago.

'Time to pay the fiddler, you sons of bitches!' muttered Sheriff Marsh Kilgour as he and his men settled down on the low ridge surrounding the riverbank camp, the teepees shrouded in drifting night-fire smoke, hardly a soul stirring in this thick grey light, hung with rags of mist clinging to the trees. There wasn't even the usual dawning birdsong.

Marsh Kilgour worked his battered watch out from the pocket of his vest, pulled his head back to squint at the time. He couldn't read it properly but it was somewhere near five o'clock. Just light enough to pick out the special teepees where the hostages were – non-targets for now.

Kilgour rolled onto his belly again, and drew the rifle butt tight into this shoulder. 'Welcome to your last day on earth, Yaller Wolf, you woman-snatchin' son of a bitch!'

He opened fire and a second later guns crashed from all round the ridges. These were not warning shots – right from the first bullet, they were meant to kill. They shredded the warriors' teepees, scattered smouldering cooking fires, bullets cutting through buffalo-hide shields hanging by entrances with the warriors' weapons. Horses on the picket line were slaughtered where they stood, fell writhing and shrieking and kicking. Two boys were the first Indians to die, running in terror from their teepee. They never knew who was attacking or why they were cut down before they had taken two steps outside the teepee. Young bodies were flung into violent contortions by the scything bullets.

By then men and women were running out, bewildered by the sudden and unexpected attack. Children screamed and fled in panic – only to be ridden down by the first wave of attackers charging in on mane-flying, wild-eyed horses, guns hammering mercilessly. Morg O'Day sat astride his big Arab black, shotgun thundering, buckshot shredding two braves who ran at him with tomahawks raised. He flung the gun from him, wanting something he didn't have to stop and reload every couple of shots, slid his Henry repeater from the saddle scabbard. Lever and trigger worked in a blur and he moved the barrel from red man to red man, killing without thought or feeling.

By now the horsemen had been joined by the men who had been shooting from the ridge and there were hand-to-hand fights with muscular Indians, using stone clubs, hatchets, butts of heavy but empty trade rifles to attack or defend. The blood of white and Indian stained the ground. Men roared their death-cries to the morning sun as it flooded over the Saltlicks.

Morgan leapt from the saddle, having seen a bunch of women running into teepees built in a half-circle around one that was taller and more decorated with commemorative battle pictures than the rest. There was a yellow wolf's head painted on one of the sloping sides above the entrance flap.

Morg glanced around. He was flanked by grim-faced men from the valley, looking for Indians to kill – but also, hopefully, for some sign of family members or loved ones who had been taken in that treacherous raid five years before... They began calling names.

'Edith! 'Tis Zeke, my love! Are you here...?'

'Lila Henderson! Lila Henderson! D'you still remember your old pa...? Little Lila...?'

'Donny! Donny, boy! It's Renn, your

brother! I've come to take you home, Donny... Ma's pinin' for you...'

The men were shouting, some with sobs in their voices, making so much noise it was hard to understand their words. But Morgan O'Day's bellow drowned out the others:

'Katy Blaine! Katy Blaine! – I've come for you, dear Kate! And I'll not leave without you – nor without seein' your tormentor on his way to hell! You know who it is, Katy! I kept my word! I said I'd find you no matter how long it took, and here I am! Where are you? Give me a sign!'

He was surprised to hear a woman's voice weakly call his name from the door flap of the big tent with the wolf's head painted on it. He glimpsed a sun-browned arm and a buckskin fringe and then he was charging through, discarding his emptied rifle, snatching out his Colt pistol as he dived in, somersaulting and rolling, hoping the percussion caps hadn't come adrift from the cylinder's nipples.

He glimpsed her – torn buckskin dress, dark with blood, flung in a heap against one wall like discarded laundry. She was sobbing and her hair was matted and–

Yellow Wolf came hurtling across the dim interior, hatchet raised in one hand, knife in the other. If he had been able to stifle his roar of triumph, he might have killed Morgan O'Day. But the big rancher heard his choked-off cry, whirled, and the massive Indian with the wolfskin headgear spilling its cape over his wide shoulders was no more than a yard from him, tomahawk already descending. A giant of a man who had led his warriors on bloody raids ranging far and wide for ten years – magnificent and murderous...

Morg ducked and twisted, fell awkwardly. But his gun hand was free and as the Indian reared above him, he put four shots into him. The bullets climbed from the man's breech-clout, up across his belly and into his barrel chest. He dropped to his knees, still trying to use the hatchet. The woman hurled herself onto the Indian's back, clawing at his eyes with broken, dirt-clogged nails. Yellow Wolf thrust her from him and twisted towards Morg. The rancher triggered his last two shots. One misfired, but the other smashed into the Indian's head, exploding it like a rotten melon.

The rancher kicked the body aside, knelt beside the woman, cradling her against his chest, wincing when he saw her wounds: knife-slashes and two bullet holes. He groaned in anguish: *What kind of a God did this to a man?* his reeling mind screamed inside his head, as her blood soaked through his shirt.

'M-Mor-gan!' she whispered, skeletal fingers clawing weakly at his sweat-soaked shirt. 'You – came...'

'Gave you my word, Katy!' *Christ, she was hard to understand, almost like she'd forgotten how to speak English.*

He glanced at the dead Yellow Wolf and curled his lip: *too bad the bastard was past suffering!*

But, now, after all this time! Just when he had found her again, had her in his arms – she was dying. It would be all over in a few minutes... It had all been for nothing. The years of torment and worry, the endless searching that had seen a dozen fine horses die under him, ridden into the desert sand or the sun-baked canyons, the killer alkali wastes … and a score of good men had found lonely graves in the forlorn, wind-scoured canyons of Yellow Wolf's home country – now, all-for-nothing!

# CHAPTER 1

## QUICKSAND

The sun was standing a hand's-breadth-and-a-half above the western peaks of the sawtooths when Blaine rode upriver and found Hardesty asleep under a tree.

Not ten yards away, the cattle in his charge were bellowing and snorting and struggling in quicksand that was already up to their bellies.

Hardesty's awakening was not gentle.

A hard, scuffed-toe riding boot bent in his ribs on his left side, rolled him out of the shade into the burning sun. Grunting and already swearing, he came abruptly out of his doze and crouched, hugging himself as he blinked up at the tall manshape standing over him.

'What the hell...?'

Blaine kicked him again alongside the ear, not hard enough to put him out, but with plenty of force to send him sprawling off the bank into the shallows. Clem Hardesty roared and erupted out of the muddy water, clambering up the bank, running in at Blaine, head down, arms out-stretched, eager to grapple and fight.

But Blaine had other ideas. He twisted aside, slapped one reaching arm away, grabbed Hardesty's long black hair and threw him against the tree. He cannoned off and went down to one knee, holding his throbbing head. He snapped it up quickly enough when he heard the whisper of gun metal against leather. Blaine, dark, wolfish face totally deadpan, those grey-green eyes looking almost dead, thrust the Colt's muzzle against Hardesty's teeth as he cocked the hammer.

'We'll settle our differences later – right now, you get your rope and mount up. We're gonna save as many of those cows as we can.'

Clem Hardesty's thick lips curled, but then he frowned, shifted his gaze past the long, rangy shape of Blaine. He noticed the cows' predicament for the first time and his jaw dropped.

'Judas priest! I – I never...' His words were slurred because of the gun pressing against his lips.

'You never did the job you were s'posed to,' cracked Blaine coldly, grinding with the gun muzzle. Hardesty wrenched his head aside, spitting a little blood.

'Get that thing outta my face!'

Blaine tapped him across the temple and Hardesty swayed, cursing, crabbing away on all fours, fear showing in his eyes now. Blaine's boot found his backside and as Hardesty sprawled, the tall man yanked the coiled rope off the saddlehorn and flung it at him.

'Get going, Clem, or I'll shoot you right here.'

Hardesty groped for the rope, standing slowly and unsteadily. His face was contorted with hate. 'Yeah, we'll settle this, all right!'

Between them, they saved seven out of the ten steers, tossing ropes over the long curved horns, using the range-trained mounts to help drag the beasts on to solid footing. Of the other three, one was already down to the chest and floundering in panic, driving its body deeper into the ooze. The other two were in too far to save.

Blaine's Winchester '66 blasted, just the three shots necessary, then he turned the smoking muzzle on to the sweating Hardesty who stiffened, wet rope dangling from one hand.

'Wade out and put your rope on the nearest cow,' Blaine ordered. 'No sense in wasting good beef; we'll butcher it on the bank and send out a buckboard to bring in the meat.'

'S'pose you do it,' Hardesty said slowly, face challenging. 'I'm about plumb-tuckered.'

'After the way you were sleeping when I found you?' Blaine shook his head slowly, but he sheathed the rifle and swung down from his mount. 'You're just bone lazy, Clem. You've been warned. This time it's the finish for you. Only you ain't just going to ride in and collect your time and head on out, you're gonna remember your time here at Broken Wheel.'

Hardesty bared yellow-stained teeth. 'I sure will. But no damn breed's gonna try to whip me...'

'This one is gonna *do* it,' Blaine murmured as he walked forward. The 'breed' part didn't bother him: that's what he was and there was nothing he could do about it and he had learned long ago how futile it was to go through life bristling and getting into fights just to protest. So he could live with being called a breed.

But what galled him was he knew Hardesty meant it as a bad kind of insult and he was damned if he'd let this lazy sonuver feel good at his expense for any reason.

Clem Hardesty tossed the wet coils of rope into Blaine's face but the tall man batted the rope aside, stepped in as the other charged. Clem shuddered as a fist banged against his jaw and knocked him sideways. He staggered and came back swinging, found the blow blocked by an uplifted forearm and then felt the smashing impact of a fist driving into his midriff.

His legs wobbled and he floundered, grabbing instinctively at Blaine. His wild, uncoordinated efforts fouled the tall man's flurry of blows and although they landed, Hardesty was too close for them to do much damage. Blaine twisted and thrust him off, then pulled him back while he was still off-balance, snapped his head up and kneed him in the belly.

Hardesty bared his teeth, sucking in desperately needed air violently as a tattoo of punches mauled him. He managed to hit back, throwing two good blows into the hard-muscled midriff of Blaine. The tall man was in good shape and took them without effect. Hardesty, a saloon brawler from way back, bored in, swinging confidently but wildly.

Suddenly his head snapped back on his

shoulders and his view of the mountains and river and trees, was scrambled violently, tinged with red. He felt himself staggering as if falling off the world, then came up against a bunched fist at the end of an iron-hard forearm. He felt as if his spine had been driven through his back. He tumbled wildly into whirling space.

When he opened his eyes, groaning with even that small effort, his vision took a little time to focus and what he saw did nothing to make, him feel any better. Blaine was sitting close by, broad back against the tree, smoking a cigarette down.

'Ready to butcher that steer now?' he asked, stubbing out the butt against a tree root.

Hardesty groaned, then, as he began to come slowly to life, he cursed, sat up stiffly.

'Morg's gonna hear about this,' he gasped, swollen and split lips slurring his words.

'Sure, when you go to draw your time.'

Hardesty froze, 'You cain't fire me!'

'I'm doing it, Clem. We butcher that steer, then we drive the others back to the spread. Someone brings a buckboard out to collect the meat, and you ride on out. That's twice I've told you. It better be enough.'

Hardesty thought about it. 'We'll see what

Luke has to say!'

'Don't matter who you run to, won't do you no good. Now let's get this chore done.'

From the porch, Morgan O'Day watched the Mexican cookhouse roustabout, the one they called Fernando, harness a team to a buckboard and drive out of the ranchyard through the long shadows of late afternoon. But it was idle observation: his real interest was in Clem Hardesty, battered and moving mighty stiffly, talking earnestly with his son, Lucas, down by the barn. *Someone had been in a fight ... a hard fight!* Morg observed silently.

His gaze wandered across to the corrals where Blaine was unsaddling his sweat-polished sorrel. He, too, was moving a little stiffly and his lean face showed a couple of signs of violence. Not as bad as Hardesty's which told the old rancher plenty.

Then Lucas came hurrying across the yard while Clem Hardesty limped to the washbench at the rear of the bunkhouse. Lucas was medium tall, average build, and liked to dress in work clothes that others might figure were good enough to wear into town for a Saturday night on the tiles. He was twenty-seven years old, a good worker – if he had plenty of men he could delegate the manual labour to – and good with the ranch's books. But he lacked something, always had...

Morgan, deep down, knew what it was, but wasn't about to admit that his son was weak, bordering on being a coward, even to himself... But he was his son and so Morg was willing to overlook his faults. But he kind of wished Lucas O'Day had a little of Blaine's steel in his backbone and the breed's sense of right and wrong and... *Hell! A man had to love his children, didn't he? No matter what...*

Now Lucas came up onto the porch, his handsome, well-fed face flushed, clean shaven so close the skin gleamed and never seemed to sweat. He pushed back his hat, revealing tight black curls that sprang down on to his forehead as he turned worried brown eyes to his father.

'Pa, Blaine's in some kind of a tizzy over Clem. Told him he's fired.'

'What kinda tizzy?'

Lucas shrugged. 'Nothing much – Clem had worked his butt off getting those steers out of the brush above the riverbend, turned 'em out to graze a spell while he took a smoke. He was that tuckered he fell asleep. Blaine come in like a high wind outta the north, cracked a couple of his ribs, then beat him up...'

'For fallin' asleep on the job?' queried the older O'Day.

Lucas pursed his womanish lips and shrugged. 'Couple of the cows'd wandered upstream a little and went into the river...'

Morg sat straighter in his chair. 'At the *high* bend? Where the quicksand is...?'

Lucas nodded briefly, trying to play down the seriousness of this. 'There was plenty of graze for 'em where Clem left 'em.' Lucas licked his lips. 'But, Pa, Clem can't be blamed for that! He said it was hell busting those steers outta that brush in the saw-tooths. You know what it's like up there... Pa, he's a pretty good cowpoke. We can't let him go just because he knocked himself out for the ranch and fell asleep. Hell, he only sat down for a smoke. He never *meant* to doze off... And they saved seven cows outta the ten, butchered one of the dead ones... Fernie's gone to collect the meat now.'

Morgan looked down to where Blaine was hanging his saddle across the top corral rail. 'Tell Blaine I want to see him.'

Lucas smiled. 'Sure, Pa! Can I tell Clem he's still drawing pay?'

'Send Blaine up to me.'

Lucas went away whistling. He knew he

had talked his father around – hell, he'd had plenty of practice over the years. Why, he was even better at swinging things his way than was Kitty, and she could turn many a man to water with just a roll or two of those hazel eyes with the fluttering dark lashes...

'The Old Man wants you up to the porch,' Lucas said as Blaine headed for the wash bench.

The tall man turned and looked soberly at his half-brother. 'You wag your tail and let your tongue hang out on behalf of that son of a bitch Hardesty?'

Lucas flushed. 'No need for that! I'm the one has to see the ranch makes a profit and we can't do that if we start firing our top hands in the middle of round-up.'

Blaine looked hard at Lucas. 'You figure Hardesty for a top hand and I'm Governor of California.'

Lucas flushed, moved uneasily. 'Anyway, you don't have the clout to fire the men here without first referring to me or Pa, Blaine!'

Lucas swung away, flushing but smiling to himself, too: that was as good a chance as he'd ever had of putting that damn breed in his rightful place...!

Blaine paused at the foot of the porch steps,

one boot on the bottom tread. He thumbed back his hat, showing sweat-darkened hair. The sun threw a shadow of his hawklike nose across one bruised cheek.

'You beat up on Clem pretty bad, looks like,' opined Morgan. 'But I see he got in a lick or two.'

Blaine shrugged. 'He riled me. Seems to think he can do what he likes – him and that pard of his, Clint Rendell. They're both pains in the butt.' He squinted at O'Day. 'I've seen you favour 'em from time to time, too.'

Morgan's face hardened and he shook a stiff finger in Blaine's direction. 'You watch it! You don't talk to me like that!'

Blaine said nothing, his face unreadable. Morg let his breathing settle and said in a milder tone, 'Clem's a good man, even if he is a mite lazy. He's worked for me for ten years. Likely feels he has a right to cut a few corners.'

'You're the one pays his wages.'

O'Day's mouth tightened into a thin slash beneath his drooping frontier moustache. He sighed. 'You just don't give a damn, do you?'

'I give a damn – where it matters.'

'And who decides that?'

Blaine merely held the old man's gaze. 'So what happens? Hardesty stays?'

23

Morg hadn't really made up his mind when he had sent for Blaine but now he nodded curtly: *Damn, Blaine! The man was just too hard for his own good at times. If he hadn't given his word all those years ago, he might've…*

'Yeah, I'm willin' to give him another chance. And that means you are, too. He's just another cowboy, but I'd watch him if I was you, Blaine. Clem Hardesty's got a long memory – and one of the things he won't forget is that you beat-up on him, and left him marked for all the others to see.'

'Luke tell you we saved seven, and butchered one of the downers?'

'He told me. You keepin' pace with the round-up times? We can't miss that drive or we're in real trouble – Bank's puttin' on the pressure for a mortgage payment. I held out last time, borrowed more money to fence in them extra acres takin' in Fool's Canyon. But Hayden won't stand for it this year.'

'Use your influence. He's Marsh Kilgour's brother-in-law, ain't he…?'

Morg's eyes narrowed. 'Don't make no nevermind – Marsh, I get along with. His sister, Abigail, never forgave me for marryin' Gracie instead of her. She'll influence Miles Hayden if it means makin' things hard for me.'

'You've made too many enemies over the years, Morg.'

He never called O'Day 'Pa' like Lucas and Kitty, Morgan's blood children, did. When Morgan had told him he was only part of the O'Day family because of his benevolence, he had specifically said, *'Now you know your place, you can quit callin' me "Pa". You're twelve year old, no real kin, so you can call me Morgan... I ain't your real father: he's dead. And you might's well know, I was the one killed him...'*

Blaine had never called O'Day 'Pa' since that landmark day, thirteen years ago.

And never would.

'Before she died in my arms, your Ma – my dear Katy – told me she had a four old son, fathered by that red devil, Yellow Wolf. She got me to promise with her last breath I'd raise you and take care of you for the rest of your life– It's a promise I'll keep. But you'll never have my name and you'll never be called "Adam" like she named you in this family. Katy married a man called Blaine because of family pressures, but we both knew we had been meant for each other. She never broke faith with Blaine and I never tried to make her. And I stayed true to Gracie till she died... I'm damned if I'll use your Injun name and while it churns my

25

belly, "Blaine's" what you'll be called within my hearin' from now on. It'll be a constant reminder of my promise to Katy... Man, I loved that woman so! If only we'd...'

But he'd said enough that day.

'I'll work hard for you, Morgan,' the boy had said flatly. 'I'll give you your money's worth.'

It was a cold, cocky tone, almost contemptuous. O'Day had flushed with anger then, came close to slapping that dark, narrowly-handsome face.

'That don't enter into it!' he snapped. 'I don't give my word lightly – to anyone!'

'Nor I, you've taught me that much.'

O'Day still could call up the way the child-Blaine had stared back at him. Face narrow and sober, the eyes disturbing and un-flinching, looking at him the way he looked at every white man and woman with that same stubborn pride and 'don't-push-me-around' contempt that Morgan O'Day knew he had inherited from Yellow Wolf.

At times he woke sweating in the night, wondering what else Blaine might have inherited from that savage.

# CHAPTER 2

## REVENGE

Round-up was almost over and the final branding and preparations for the trail drive were proceeding well, when Kitty O'Day came back to Broken Wheel from her College For Young Ladies in St Louis for the summer break.

Morgan had seen that she was named 'Catherine' but while Gracie was an easy-going wife, and knew she had been married on the rebound, she drew the line at calling her daughter 'Katy': it would be too much of a reminder of her husband's unrequited love for Katy Blaine. She had insisted that everyone call the baby girl Kitty and Morgan had let her have her way – there were some whirlpools in his conscience about the way he had treated Gracie from time to time, knowing he had made a convenience of her after Katy had been forced into her marriage with Adam Blaine. Who, when you got right down to it and, in some private moments,

Morgan allowed, was not so bad, and had likely taken Katy as wife when he would have preferred some other woman. (Morgan was wrong there – Adam Blaine had loved Katy truly and ended up dying for her to prove it so, when he had stepped into the path of a bullet meant for her during a stage hold-up.) Not that it mattered now – that had been nigh on twenty years ago...

Kitty had inherited all Gracie's good looks, was a long-legged, coltish kind of girl, although she was now twenty-two years of age, a couple of years younger than Blaine. She knew Blaine was interested in her but while she was virtually the only white person he ever smiled at – or laughed with – he was careful to hide any show of affection from Morgan and Lucas or anyone else. She was also 'interested' in Blaine but after being with some of the other 'young ladies' at Madame Le Charme's college she sometimes teased him. The older 'young ladies' had assured her this was the thing to do, and while she enjoyed it in one way, she was always kind of sad when she saw how he tried to hide the small hurt he felt each time.

She was a breezy, bright young woman, and every man who worked on Broken Wheel worshipped her, and kept an inconspicuous eye on her when she rode alone on the range or into a part of the large ranch they considered held danger of any kind.

Kitty knew this and found it gave her a quiet thrill to know so many tough men were doing this on her behalf. One of her friends at college, Miss Christina McGovern, of the Colorado McGoverns (discoverers and owners of the richest gold mine in the Territory) told her that what she felt was a thrill of power.

'Don't be silly, Christy!'

Christina was far more sophisticated and worldly than Kitty O'Day – even told Kitty in confidence that she had slept with two different men, one almost as old as her father – and she assured her that it was indeed *power* that thrilled her so. 'Women can control men, make them do whatever they want – just let them have their way occasionally to keep them happy and a young lady can go through life with everything she desires.'

'Oh, Christy, that's – that's an awful thing to say! If Madame heard you...'

'Pooh on Madame!' Christina said recklessly, and showed Kitty the sapphire pendant she wore close to her breast beneath the mandatory choke-collar that was part of the college dress. 'It's set in gold on a gold chain

29

– my latest beau gave it to me.'

Kitty admired it but flushed as she said, 'I'm afraid to ask what you had to – do – to get it.'

Christina laughed, pushed her friend's shoulder gently. 'You know darn well – and I like it, so where's the harm?'

'But – when you get married. Your husband will – want you – pure!'

'D'you think I don't know how to act like a virgin? There's nothing simpler, Kitty O'Day. You should grow up – you can't be a child forever...'

'Well, I think perhaps I'll stay a "child" a little longer...'

But Christina McGovern had aroused a certain curiosity in Kitty that made her blush even when she was alone and she allowed herself to think of how it must be for a man and woman to be together...

As usual, Blaine saddled the grey, dappled Arab for Kitty on the first morning she was home and had it waiting when she appeared on the porch of the big log and riverstone ranch house. He had his black saddled, too, and was disappointed to see Kitty was not wearing her riding clothes.

'Your horse awaits, lady,' Blaine said and anyone else hearing him use such levity would stop dead in their tracks. For Blaine was known as a sober man, rarely smiling, taking life very seriously.

'Oh, hello, Blaine.' Kitty gave him a smile, warm enough, but fleeting. She seemed distracted in some way, looking beyond him to the activity in the pastures where the herd was gathering. 'You'll be going on the drive, I suppose.'

He nodded, eyes watching her closely now, bringing a slight flush to her cheeks. 'Couple of days and we'll be on the trail – doesn't give us much time. Are you coming for our usual ride...?'

She hesitated, let her hazel eyes slide to him and just as quickly away. 'I – don't really feel like riding today, Blaine – I'll leave it, I think – but don't unsaddle Sunny. I may go a little later.'

Disappointment was plain on his face but he covered quickly. 'I'll tether him in the shade – later, we have to get the trail brands on the last bunch and tomorrow Morgan wants me to burn a firebreak on the ridge. Day after, we'll be headin'-'em-up and startin' for railhead...'

Her look and tone softened. 'I – I'm sorry, Blaine– But, truly, I'm not feeling all that well this morning. In fact, I've been off-colour for a couple of weeks now – I'll see you before you go.'

He hesitated. 'You'll be gone back to college before the trail drive's over.'

She nodded. 'I said I'm sorry, Blaine! There's nothing I can do about it!'

She turned abruptly and went into the house. He frowned, started to lead the Arab towards the trees and shade. He scowled when he saw Clem Hardesty carrying a pack frame and straps crossing the yard, the man grinning from ear-to-ear, his bruises and swellings giving his face a lopsided look.

'What's funny?' Blaine asked quietly.

Hardesty stopped. 'You dunno? You don't recognize the brush-off when a gal gives it to you?' He shook his head, still chuckling. 'Oh, man! You got plenty to learn about women! She's got herself a boyfriend back East, bet my britches on it.'

'Get on with your chores, Clem,' Blaine told him mildly and tethered the horse under the tree. 'You're lucky to still have a job.'

But he threw a puzzled look towards the house before he started for the corrals where his own horse waited patiently.

He rode out towards the pastures and Lucas, sitting at a portable table set up under some cotton-woods, called him across.

'Blaine, I want you to check my count–'

Blaine took the heavy, leather-bound tally book, glanced at Lucas. 'Down much?'

'That's just it – I make it almost a hundred more than we expected.'

'Hell, Hardesty and Rendell were s'posed to cut out any cows from the other spreads three days back.'

Lucas shook his head. 'They're not to blame – I checked with them. They said they did the job, all right.'

'I'll believe that when I see for myself.' He swung into saddle and lifted his reins, but before setting the black moving, asked casually, 'You notice Kitty's not so bright this time home?'

Lucas frowned slightly as he glanced up. 'Oh? Well, who knows with women? Specially young snooty ones like my sister – I'd like to know what *really* goes on at those so-called "Ladies Colleges".'

Creases cut two knife-strokes between Blaine's grey-green eyes. 'What's that mean?'

Lucas made an impatient gesture. 'Oh, you know – young women away from home. Slippin' out from the dorm at night. Hell, I used to do it all the time when Pa sent me to Cattleman's College in Austin... There's a "Young Gentleman's" School just down the street from where Kitty goes – wouldn't be surprised if she's got a boyfriend.'

He looked sharply at Blaine: he had been talking idly, half his mind on his books, but saw now that Blaine was seriously worried and Lucas couldn't resist twisting the knife he had unintentionally plunged into his half-brother. 'Likely had some kind of lovers' tiff. She'll get over it... Er, I think Alamo's waiting for you to help with that branding...'

Blaine wheeled the black without a word and rode swiftly towards the herd and the impatient figure of Alamo Ames, Morgan's trail boss...

The burn-back was a hot, filthy job and it seemed to be one of the hottest days Blaine could recall. He had brought a couple of hands with him and a buckboard carrying casks of river water and several pails – just in case the fire got out of control.

There was a rising wind, and its breath was like the blast from the maw of a furnace. Blaine had told Morgan it might be best to wait for a calmer day but O'Day was adamant.

'You'll be off on the drive tomorrow or the next day – you're good at burn-backs, Blaine. I want that ridge cleared into a firebreak before you leave. If it was to go in a brushfire, it'd jump the river easily and sweep right on up here to the house. Besides, burnin' off over-growth'll give the grass a chance to grow through and we'll have useable pasture for the herds... Indians know the benefit of burnin' back.'

Blaine didn't argue but he saw the shrewd look in the Old Man's grey eyes. It wasn't often he reminded Blaine of his ancestry but when he did, he was never subtle about it ... even if he believed he was.

It was a hell of a job, kept him and his two helpers on the run for hours and finally he had to send down for more men. The wind's direction had changed and the fire was sweeping towards the river. If the wind kept working around to the north it would lend the flames enough impetus to leap the river and reach the home pastures.

His clothes were singed and ragged, his skin blistered here and there, a couple of places with burned flesh showing redly. His eyes stung and his throat was hoarse with a hacking rawness. His lungs felt hot and he was dizzy. Two of the other men had passed out with the heat and had to be doused with water. Smoke drifted down towards the herds and set the cows into restless bawling.

Blaine figured they had most of the fire under control now and sent back the two men who had passed out to help Alamo and the others.

The other two cowboys were in singed rags just like Blaine and he told them they could tip the last of the cask water onto the fire and then go back to the ranch for lunch and clean-up.

'I'm gonna wash-up in the river, and make sure there's no slow-burns left on the bank–'

The men departed and he made his way down the blackened, smouldering slopes to the river, walking along a half mile each way to check there were no sparks or hot embers. He found a couple of suspect places, stepped into the muddy river and scooped handfuls of water over them.

Looking around, back up the blackened slope of the ridge, he studied it for a few minutes then tore off the remains of his shirt, bunched it up and flung it onto the bank. He sat down, pulled off his boots and drained the river water out of them, then stripped off his trousers and waded out knee deep. He sat on the gravelly bottom, scooped up handfuls of coarse sand and scrubbed his body and arms and legs, rubbed hard at his face with water only, dousing his head a dozen times and shaking his thick black hair out of his eyes and ears.

With water still dripping from him as he sat there, he started to rise, then froze. He had heard something.

Holding a breath, ignoring the soft trickling sounds of the river and the birdsong on the far bank where the trees had been untouched by the flames, he strained to hear that alien sound again. *There it was!*

He felt his glowing skin prickle with a flood of goosebumps. *It was someone sobbing – body-wracking sobs deep and terrible and hurting.*

He would rather it had been the soft grunt of a mountain lion stalking him. That was something he knew he could handle ... but this! A woman crying!

Well, it was no business of his, that was for sure. He could just ignore it...

'The hell you think you're kidding?' he murmured, standing and heading for his soot-streaked trousers with the ragged holes burned in the cloth in a dozen places. They were awkward to pull on while he was wet and he only buttoned up some of the fly. He took his six gun from its holster where he had hung it on the saddlehorn and, heart hammering – harder than it would have if it *had* been a lion he had heard – he made his way around some jutting rocks.

And found the person who was sobbing so brokenheartedly.

It did nothing for his ease to recognize Kitty O'Day, sitting on a rock a few feet above the river, face streaked and red with her crying, body shuddering with the spasms. But what really chilled him was the flash of sunlight on the long blade of the hunting knife she held pressed between her breasts.

'Kitty! For God's sake!'

The words tore from him and he waded towards her even as she snapped up her head and the moist, reddened eyes widened as she saw him tucking the Colt into his partially fastened waistband.

She leapt up, swaying, missed her footing and fell. He saw the knife slip from her hand, splash into the water, and he did his best to catch her, but her weight bore him down into the shallows. He threw his arms about her in an effort to stop her wild thrashing and she struggled with a strength he didn't know any young woman could possess.

'Stop it!' he gritted. 'Kitty, stop this! For Chrissakes, girl, what – the *hell* d'you think – you're doing...?'

She tried to bite him and it startled him. He had never seen such a – a *mad, crazy* look in her eyes. He would never have recognized her. Her breasts heaved against his hands and he didn't even notice his grip was covering them. The girl got one arm free, slashed at his face, and fingernails gouged streaks in his flesh.

'Let – me – *go!* You – you're like all of – them! I hate you! I – hate – all – men!'

'Calm down!' Blaine stood, having the advantage now, and he pinned her down with one knee, fought to control her slashing hands as she beat at him, bearing her back relentlessly against the bank.

Lucas heard the horse racing in hard and glanced up from his books under the cottonwood, frowning and standing quickly. He recognized Clem Hardesty rowelling his mount, lashing at it with his quirt, his swollen lips drawn back from his teeth. He reined down and started yelling before the horse had stopped skidding.

'The river!' Clem panted, pointing behind him. 'Alamo sent me down to tell – Blaine to hurry up...' He swallowed, fighting for breath. 'He's there – with Miss Kitty! He's half-nekked and her blouse is all wet and half torn off– Looks like he's tryin' to – rape her!'

Lucas felt a cold knot tightening in his

belly, as it always did at some unexpected news of a disaster he would have to do something about... Then it passed and the rage at the thought of that half-breed Blaine trying to rape his sister shook him violently.

'Send someone for Morgan– Then you bring Clint Rendell and any others you can grab and lead me to the river!'

He reached for his six gun, knowing he would never use it, but making the visible gesture. Hardesty was already swinging away, smiling crookedly.

*'You're in real trouble this time, breed!'* he murmured and called to Clint Rendell who was riding up to see what all the hurry was about.

By now, Blaine had some measure of control over the hysterical girl. She had calmed down to the point where she was no longer trying to tear his eyes out but she was still sobbing uncontrollably and it took him some time to make out what she was saying as she clung to him.

'Oh – Blaine! I'm so – ashamed! Father will kill me! When he finds out!'

He recalled the knife then, its blade poised between her breasts over her heart. He felt chilled.

'What the hell can it be, Kitty, to make you – want to kill yourself? That's what you were going to do, isn't it?'

She nodded miserably. 'I – I couldn't work up the – courage to push the knife in...'

'Thank God for that – but – why...?' She shook her head, muttered 'I'm too ashamed!' and he shook her, making her look up at him. 'Kitty – I dunno what it is, but it doesn't matter. I'll help you whatever your problem – just – tell me – so I'll know what to do...'

She almost smiled for a brief moment, lifted one shaking hand to stroke his gouged cheek. 'Oh, look what I've done to you!... I – I should've known you'd be the one to – understand, Blaine – forgive me...'

'You don't have to ask my forgiveness for anything, Kitty – I thought you knew that.'

She nodded, still sniffling. 'Yes – there – there's this girl at College – Christina McGovern. She's kind of boy crazy and she – took me to a party. We – sneaked out of dorm and went to this – party at the Young Gentleman's School–' She paused, snorted. *'Young Gentlemen!* They don't know the meaning of the word – they – they put some – alcohol in my fruit juice, kept doing it. I – didn't know till too late – and–' She choked off unable to go on but he gentled her and stroked her stringy, sand-clogged hair and she blurted it all out so that she had finished speaking for some seconds before he had separated the words and taken their meaning. 'One of the boys seduced me and now I find I'm pregnant and Father will disown me at best, kill me at worst! I'm so – afraid and – ashamed, Blaine! The shame is the worst, I think...'

He pulled her against him but she started to panic again and began to beat at his shoulders as he said desperately, 'You don't have to worry about anything, Kitty! I'll take care of you – Your father doesn't have to know anything about this. No one need ever know. I – I'll marry you and we'll...'

*'Like hell you will!'*

They leapt apart as a bunch of men charged out of the brush and swept on to the river bank, a raging, mad-eyed Morgan O'Day in the lead, a gloating Lucas and Clem Hardesty only a pace or two behind.

# CHAPTER 3

## PUNISHMENT

Once, when Blaine was eleven years old, he had saddled Morgan's bay Arab when the rancher was out on the range, working mavericks with a crew of cowhands. Lucas warned him he was taking a big risk. A *mighty* big risk...

'Pa'll never know unless you tell him.' Blaine, at that time, still believed Morgan was his real father and that Lucas and Kitty were his brother and sister. It was only after he turned twelve that Morgan O'Day told him of his true background.

'He said no one is to ride that horse but him,' Lucas said smugly. *'No* one!'

'Oh, don't be so stuffy, Luke,' Kitty said, smiling at the hesitant Blaine – he somehow knew that Lucas would eventually spill the beans, but Kitty's words helped decide him to ride the Arab now. 'Go on, Blaine – I'll see that Luke doesn't tell Dad. If he does – well, I'm sure I'll have no trouble finding something that Luke has done that he shouldn't have… All right, Brother Dear?'

Blaine gave Kitty a brief smile and climbed on to the lower rung of the corral fence so he could reach the stirrup, then floundered his way into the saddle on the tall thoroughbred stallion. He touched his heels to the glistening flanks, flicked the reins and the Arab was away, accelerating to full speed, knowing there was a lightweight stranger in the saddle. The cowboys didn't refer to the Arab as 'Devil Horse' for nothing.

It went like the wind and after Blaine got his breath and he had lost his hat, he threw back his head and howled a cry that he didn't know till many years later was the victory call of a Comanche after he had succeeded in taming a wild mustang.

The Arab streaked across the pasture, Kitty waving encouragement, Lucas holding his breath, half-hoping something would happen to Blaine.

He got his wish.

The horse stepped into a gopher hole, snapped the fetlock like a stalk of celery and Blaine travelled through the air for a measured fifteen feet before landing in juniper bushes. He lost some hide and tore his shirt and trousers, but, limping, bleeding from the nose, he ran to the floundering Arab that was shrilling in its agony, staggering as it tried to stand firm on three legs, occasionally lowering the useless dangling right foot but immediately raising it again as soon as it touched the ground.

Kitty was in tears, frozen, unable to move, one hand at her mouth, knowing full well what dreadful punishment was now awaiting Blaine. Lucas knew, too, but he smiled slyly.

'I won't *have* to tell Pa anything now!' he said and Kitty recovered enough to turn to him and sob, 'I *hate* you. Lucas O'Day! I wish you weren't my brother, you miserable sneak!'

Names never hurt Lucas, least of all any that his younger sister called him. Morgan O'Day called him a few names, too, when he rode back from the maverick round-up. But he didn't waste time: he shot the Arab humanely, then ordered Blaine tied to the corral fence, and took down the buggy whip.

It was Alamo Ames, the Broken Wheel wrangler at that time, who tore Blaine's shirt down to his waist. He also gave the boy a strip of doubled harness leather to bite on. Blaine turned his head as Morgan shook out the whip's lash and ordered Kitty and Lucas to be taken to the house. He drew back his right arm and froze when his gaze locked with the boy's.

Morgan was shocked at the deadly menace in the young face, the flat eyes that sent a chill through his whole body. Then Blaine spoke and even his voice sounded different, more mature, like a young man's, and bleak as a mid-winter blizzard.

'Touch me with that whip and I'll kill you some day.'

Alamo Ames was stunned. 'Don't make it worse, boy!' he said softly, watching his boss. The shock shook him as he saw how pale Morgan's face was, how tight his lips and how hollow his cheeks had suddenly become. The hand that held the whip was trembling and, amazed, Alamo saw it start to lower.

Then, abruptly, Morgan's expression changed to one of outraged determination. The lash sang and slashed across the boy's bronzed shoulders, branding the flesh forever as it split the skin and raised a welt with purple lips. The lash rose and fell four more times.

'Throw a pail of water over him to bring him round, then take him to his bunk and rub some salve into his back,' O'Day ordered, the last words trailing as he saw

Blaine's head turn slowly, spitting out the well-bitten leather, tears wetting his cheeks. But there wasn't an audible sob or groan of pain and his eyes were colder than before, if possible, but his voice was just as strong, without a quaver.

'I – warned – you,' he said.

That was all...

Now, fourteen years later, down at the river-bank, Morgan O'Day started to order Clint Rendell to go fetch his bullwhip, but his glance took in the faded, pale criss-cross scars ridging Blaine's wide, river-wet shoulders. The memory of the boy's words and his murderous look came to him again down the long years. Morgan paused, lifted his gaze to Blaine's eyes and felt the tightness in his chest.

Hardesty and Rendell were covering Blaine with their guns. Lucas was trying to quieten the screaming Kitty and another three cowboys stood around, sober-faced, waiting to see what was going to happen.

Morgan's words died within him. He cleared his throat angrily and the girl broke free of Lucas, ran to her father, screaming into his face, small fists hammering at his barrel chest.

'Leave him! Blaine did nothing! He's not the father... He was just trying to – help! *Leave him alone!*'

Morgan slapped her. One hard, numbing blow that silenced her, shocked more than hurt. She blinked, a hand touching her reddening face. Morgan wouldn't look at her. He called to Lucas.

'Take this – harlot up to the house and lock her in her room! She is to stay there, unfed, without company, until I decide what to do with her.' His voice was thick and seemed to be choking him.

'He's – done – *nothing* I tell you!' Kitty found her voice, defending Blaine, but Lucas and a cowhand took her arms roughly and dragged her away as she continued to scream her futile protests.

Morgan wouldn't meet Blaine's deadly gaze: he knew the man was remembering that time tied to the corrals with the crippled Arab shuddering its last in the hot sun... Instead of ordering Hardesty and Rendell to get his bullwhip, he said, 'Tie his hands behind his back.'

Morgan watched as Blaine stood there without resistance and managed to refrain from wincing as Hardesty pulled the ropes brutally into his flesh.

'The girl's innocent, Morgan,' Blaine said slowly. 'Give her a chance to explain–'

Morgan set bleak eyes on the half-breed. 'I'd be within my rights to shoot you dead where you stand – but I've spent a lot of time and money on you over the years because I gave my word to someone who mattered to me. I'll keep that word – and you'll continue to work for Broken Wheel. But you'll work to pay me back for all I've invested in you since I dragged you out of that stinkin' Injun cesspit where you were living – you'll work until you're too feeble or crippled to bring in an extra cent for Broken Wheel's benefit – and then I'll kick you out with only the clothes you stand in. You savvy me, mister?'

Blaine didn't flinch. That deadpan face stared back at Morgan and almost unnerved him but he forced himself to curl a lip and repeat his last words. *'Do you savvy what I said...?'*

He saw Blaine was going to speak and he began to smile coldly, but the words shocked him into silence.

'What're you going to do with Kitty?'

Even Hardesty and Rendell showed just a touch of admiration. The man had been threatened with a life-sentence of hard, unrelenting and certainly unrewarding labour – and all he could do was ask what was going to happen to Kitty!

Clem Hardesty admitted silently that that took real guts...

Morgan was flushed, then pale. He stepped forward, slapped Blaine across the face. 'Get him out of my sight – oh, and, boys, if you think it's necessary to hammer some sense into this dirty breed, you go right ahead – there'll be no complaints. As long as you leave him alive.'

Morgan turned away, shaking, sick, then thought of the daughter who had brought shame to the O'Day family and his jaw hardened and his fists curled as he strode angrily across the pasture towards the distant ranch house.

Blaine was down for the fifth time, but once again they wouldn't leave him be. Rendell, a beefy man with a large bulbous nose and blubbery lips, rubbed his aching right hand, its knuckles split and raw. He raised it to his mouth and sucked hard, spitting a little blood. 'That enough, you reckon, Clem?'

Clem Hardesty was pouring canteen water over his head and face. He was sweating, his stench making even Rendell keep his distance, and he was breathing hard, raw knuckles running with blood. He looked at his pard now through the dripping curtain of water from his heavy eyebrows.

'I'm about – winded – and my hands feel like I got 'em caught in the clothes wringer – but I ain't finished with that sonuver yet.' He stepped up to Blaine's body – hands still tied behind him – and kicked him viciously in the ribs three times.

'Remember what the Old Man said,' warned Rendell uneasily. 'Don't kill him.'

Clem spat, snarling. 'He's tough, Injun tough – he's taken more'n any whiteman I've ever beat on, but he can take a helluva lot more yet – an' he's gonna!'

He turned on Blaine again, dancing around the prone shape, kicking and stomping. Hard, breathy sounds gusted from the 'breed, blood bubbled from his nostrils and mouth. His jaw was lop-sided, his nose a purple shapeless lump. One eye was swollen and almost closed. The other seemed mostly undamaged and just as he was moving away to take a breather, Hardesty noticed this.

'Hell, he can still see! I don't want him to see anythin' when he comes round – only to *feel!* Shake the bastard up, make him wonder if we've finished with him or not...'

'Best take 'er easy, Clem,' warned Rendell who was as vicious as his pard, but he knew when to stop. Long ago he had beat a man almost to death and the Judge had told him how lucky he was not to have a hemp necktie.

'One more cowardly kick in the head and you'd be swinging from my gallows right now! Which is the rightful place for scum like you – but I'm bound by the jury's decision...' It had been a long, hard stretch in Yuma that time and Rendell was only walking around in freedom now because he had managed to escape– Of course, his name hadn't been Rendell in those days. Likely there were still wanted dodgers on him back in Arizona... So he wasn't really concerned for Blaine's welfare, only for his own.

If Blaine died at Clem Hardesty's hands – or boots – he, Clint Rendell would be charged with murder, too.

'Call it quits, Clem,' he said finally.

'When I'm good and ready!' Hardesty growled and he drew back his right foot, nudged the unconscious Blaine's head around until the right side was uppermost, then he swung the boot brutally into the eye socket, grinding...

He staggered, doubled up, gasping for

breath and Clint Rendell felt sick when he saw the bloody, mangled face of the breed.

Hardesty straightened slowly and grinned. 'Now I'm all through... Let's go get a few drinks in town to celebrate.'

'What – what about Blaine?'

Clem shrugged. 'Cut his hands free and leave him– He'll find his way to help sooner or later...'

But Rendell was deathly afraid that the man might never, move again. Even now he didn't seem to be breathing.

'You left him out there?'

Morgan O'Day glowered at the blood-spattered hardcases standing before him in the blazing sun by the corrals. His old heart was hammering as he saw the bits of flesh sticking to the toes of Hardesty's boots – *Blaine's* flesh – and, while his hatred for the breed was still strong, he felt a pang of alarm. He would later admit that he had been hurt by what he saw as Blaine's betrayal, but now he was simply shaken as his imagination ran riot and tried to picture what these fools had done to the man he had adopted as a son.

Over the years, in moments of introspection, he had admitted to himself that he cared for and admired the young man – told himself quickly that it was only because Blaine had Katy's blood flowing in his veins: he was a part of her he could still possess, even though he hated Comanche. And at least half of Blaine's blood was that of the fearsome Yellow Wolf. But he'd had the pleasure of killing that damn Injun himself, driving home the bullets with all the hatred built up over five years' of anguish, wondering about Katy's fate.

His word had been given – and to Katy herself – so he would honour it, even when he felt like killing Blaine. Which made him think about his daughter and *her* betrayal...

But right now he was facing these two hardcases and he allowed his rage to swell within him and saw them blink and cower before it.

'If that boy's dead...!'

'He ain't dead,' muttered Clint Rendell but snapped his mouth shut as Morg's gaze fell on him.

'He'll live, Morg,' Clem Hardesty said, trying to sound confident. 'You said it was OK to beat on him – long as we left him alive...'

O'Day knew he had used those words. He hadn't been thinking clearly, *couldn't* have been to give these two such latitude. Maybe he'd gone too far... But his mind was in a turmoil, what with Kitty sobbing and screaming up in her room, kicking at the door, and now seeing these two snakes spattered with Blaine's blood. Lucas seemed to be the only one in any way happy about the situation, and he was sitting astride the top corral post, pretending to write in his tally books, but listening to every word and noting every expression as Morgan tried to decide what to do about these two. He had a terrible feeling they'd killed Blaine...

'Draw your pay,' he said abruptly, seeing the shock hit Hardesty and Rendell like a slap in the face with a plate of cold mashed potato. 'There'll be a bonus, but you ride out – you're finished here.'

Rendell frowned, slow to absorb this, but Hardesty's ugly face hardened. 'We did what you *told* us to–'

'Draw your pay!'

As Morgan started to turn away, Hardesty said, 'Best be a big bonus, Morgan. We both got runaway tongues when we get a few redeyes under our belts.'

Morgan swung back and his hand dropped to his six gun butt, causing both men to stiffen and Lucas to sit up straight on the fence rail, eyes widening. But O'Day didn't draw the weapon.

'Fifty dollars apiece,' he growled, snapping at his son, 'See to it, Lucas – but first, have Alamo or someone go out and pick up Blaine. If he looks real bad – best take him into town to the doctor.'

'Marsh Kilgour's gonna want to know what happened,' Lucas said, voice shaky.

'You tell Marsh to come see me – I'll tell him what I want him to know...'

Lucas sighed, relieved, and clambered down from the fence. Hardesty and Rendell were already making for the washbench, muttering angrily.

Morgan looked up at the window of Kitty's room. He'd had planks nailed across and the room would be dark, adding to her discomfort and misery. *Good! She'd know plenty more before he was through with her...*

He was in his office, tossing down his fifth stiff whiskey when he heard the buckboard clatter into the yard. Slowly, frowning, knowing they couldn't have been to town and back yet, Morgan went to the window. His frown deepened, though it was lost amongst the weathered seams and wrinkles.

Alamo and Fernando were in the vehicle,

the Mexican driving, but there was no one in the back. A thrill of fear ran through Morgan as he dropped the empty whiskey glass and hurried to the side door, wrenching it open and striding across the yard towards the skidding buckboard.

Alamo Ames was hurrying towards him, his small, muscular figure looking tense.

'He's gone, Morg!' he called while still five yards away. 'Blood and trampled grass everywhere but he's gone...'

## CHAPTER 4

### VANISHED

They searched the river and the banks far up – and – downstream. They looked for tracks but the grass was too trampled to pick out anything in particular.

What they *didn't* find was any sign that Blaine had dragged himself to his horse and somehow managed to get into the saddle. There was enough blood staining the grass and ground for them to realise Blaine must be in a mighty bad way – lucky to be alive.

His horse was missing, too, no tracks showing.

In desperation they even searched the far side of the river but although there was a suspect place where someone or something – a horse, maybe – had quit the fast flowing waters, it was not conclusive. No other tracks were found in amongst the brush or trees there so it was dismissed.

Alamo Ames, a man with a touch of Apache in him from way back down the line of his ancestors, had been in charge of the tracking and after three hard days, rode back and reported failure to Morgan O'Day.

The rancher had changed in those three days. A man whose jet black hair had turned to silver during his late twenties – and was totally silvery-white by his early thirties – had still always managed to look fit and powerful enough for a man ten years his junior. But now his face was gaunted and he was red-eyed and Alamo smelled whiskey on his breath. His hands were even shaking a little as he packed a pipe and lit it, trying to seem casual.

'So – he's somehow beaten me. Gotten away, run with his tail between his legs.'

Alamo, medium tall and medium build, slitted his dark eyes. His face was narrow and sharp at times, at others it seemed broader, depending on his mood. Right now he was puzzled by Morgan's reaction – and appearance – but he looked quickly and hard at the rancher.

'He'd be in no fit state to get far. If he managed to roll off the bank into the river, I'd call that a minor miracle. And he'd likely drown. Those two hardcases would've given him the devil of a beatin' – dunno why you kept 'em around so long – or turned 'em loose on Blaine.'

Morgan paused as he lit his pipe, shook out the match, puffed a cloud of smoke and said, 'You've worked for me a long time, Alamo. It gives you some privileges. Don't push 'em.'

Ames wasn't fazed: he liked Blaine. Maybe it was because they both had Indian blood, or maybe it was admiration for the half-breed who had come under Morgan O'Day's reluctant care – and seemed to still be his own man.

Not like Lucas, weak and subservient to Morgan – but, in Alamo's opinion, only because he saw that one day Broken Wheel would be his if he played his cards right – and that's what he was concentrating on doing. Blaine didn't seem to think along

59

those lines, and, without saying so, did his best to make O'Day proud of him, or, at least, feel that he was getting his money's worth. With Morgan, of course, no one ever knew what his true feelings were – just like Blaine, when you got right down to it.

'As I savvy it, Kitty said Blaine had done nothin' – that he's not – the father of her child...'

'Shut up, damn you!' gritted Morgan, shaking badly now, his breathing coming hard and fast, his pipe stem snapping in his sudden convulsive grip. He stood, flung the pipe into a corner, went to the side-boy and splashed whiskey into a glass. He tossed it down, shuddered a little, had another, then, turning, snapped, 'Help yourself.'

'Later, Morg – want me to keep lookin' for Blaine?'

Morgan hesitated. 'I want you back here.'

'Well – will I send someone else out? Lucky's a good tracker...'

'Don't you worry about it! I'll decide – later.'

'Meantime, what you gonna do about Kitty?'

O'Day looked haunted, and annoyed at Alamo's prodding. He was about to snap at the man again, then his shoulders slumped and he shook his head slowly as he sat down again. 'I dunno, Alamo – I don't believe her. Blaine *has* to be the father. No one else here has shown any interest in her like Blaine. Goin' ridin', walkin'...'

'He was discreet enough. And I'd say innocent enough too.'

Morgan snorted. 'He knew I'd never approve! A half-breed courtin' my daughter! They used to go for long rides every time she came home on vacation. I should've figured sooner or later – somethin' would – happen.'

'Have you given her a chance to tell you her story?'

*'I'm not interested!* Goddammit, the girl's unmarried and pregnant! What the hell else is there to discuss? She's brought shame on my name and to make it worse, the man I showed compassion and – and kindness to has betrayed me! That's what I know – and all I need to know.'

'You're wrong – You're not being fair to either of them. If I was you...'

'Enough!' O'Day stood again, took a turn round the room, glanced at the whiskey, passed it by, but swung back and downed another stiff drink.

'That stuff's cloudin' your judgement, Morg.'

The rancher rounded swiftly. 'You've said enough – this is my family and I'll make my judgements about them. You get ready for a long ride. I've decided what I'm going to do about the girl...'

'Her name's Kitty, isn't it?'

'About the *girl*– Lucky Kinnane can start the drive. You do this chore for me then come back and catch up with him in time to take the herd into railhead and do the dickerin'.'

Alamo frowned again. 'Where you sendin' me?'

'You'll know before you leave – but take plenty of supplies. So you won't need to call into any towns along the way...'

Alamo Ames started out slowly. *Sounded to him like the Old Man didn't want anyone to know where Kitty was being sent...*

Which likely meant he was banishing her for good from Broken Wheel. It didn't set easy with Alamo Ames, but he'd been around Morgan O'Day long enough to know when to keep his mouth shut.

But this was sure one helluva thing, what had happened.

Family had always been top-of-the-list with Morg O'Day. Alamo had thought nothing could ever break that stubborn, silver-haired old buffalo.

But, by hell, this just might do it.

Kitty O'Day couldn't speak.

She had screamed so long and loudly, had hammered on the locked door of her darkened room until she had collapsed against it, half-sitting, sobbing quietly. Her throat was raw and aching from the hours she had kept trying to get her father's attention so she could explain what had really happened – how Blaine was blameless and – the rest of it.

She knew she could hardly be in any more trouble than she had already made for herself, but she wanted to try to save Blaine – even though she realised by now that Hardesty and Clint Rendell must have done their work.

She decided to write a note to her father but there wasn't enough light and he had seen to it that all letter-writing equipment was removed anyway. Even the mattress off her bed had been taken. Kitty was devastated. She had sobbed herself dry when the door finally opened and she threw an arm across her eyes as brightness slashed at her vision.

She blinked and recognized the blocky shape of Alamo Ames. He was gentle with her as he helped her to her feet. She tried to speak but only hoarse, unintelligible sounds escaped her.

'The maid'll pack a valise for you with some clothes,' the trail boss said quietly. 'Don't make a sound– Just come. Morg won't see you. You just have to come with me.'

Startled, she mouthed the question: where?

He shook his head. 'He hasn't told me yet – but a long way. Don't make it harder for yourself, Kitty. He's hurt real bad and he doesn't really know what he's doin'. Just come along and I'll do my best to try and get things straightened out when I come back.'

Her eyes widened and he knew she realised this was going to be a *lo-oo-ong* journey. She felt the flutter of her weary heart within her, the sickness churning in her stomach. Her dry lips mouthed the word and he understood.

'I don't know what's happened to Blaine, girl – Fernie and me went to pick him up in the buckboard but he was gone. No tracks that I could read – we searched the river over and over. I was afeared he must've...'

Then he stopped in mid-word. She was shaking her head vigorously. *No*, she was telling him. *He didn't go into the river...*

How could she know that? he wondered.

But more than that: she was smiling.

After another week of intense searching, even calling out men from town to help, Morgan O'Day ordered the whole thing scaled down. Hardesty and Rendell had left town, too, so no one could shed any light on what had happened to Blaine.

'He's pulled some sort of vanishin' trick, damn him!' the rancher growled and the men had the notion he was more angry at having been outsmarted than he was worried about Blaine's welfare. 'Him an' his Injun ways! Well, to hell with him! I never want to clap eyes on him again... Nor *her!*' he added and the men knew he was still hurting badly, deep and powerful...

At the end of the second week he said they couldn't delay the trail drive any longer and he ordered Lucky Kinnane to choose his men and to get the herd on the road to the railhead.

'You drive 'em carefully, don't run off the fat – I need – want the highest price I can get. If it means waitin' around a few days for Alamo to turn up, then you wait. He's the one to do the dickerin' with the meathouse agents. OK?'

Lucky said it was but he wasn't all that happy about it. It was plain Morgan didn't trust him altogether. He was a good cattle-man, had worked the big herds in north Texas before heading down here after the War. That was when he had got his nick-name – and he *had* been lucky. For a spell. A run of winning hands in trail camps and saloon back rooms, the cards falling just right. That small spread he often dreamt about looked well within reach when suddenly his luck deserted him.

Foolishly, like the desperate gambler he had become, he began doubling-up, then tripling, his bets in a frantic attempt to recoup his losses. All he did was go broke more quickly.

But the tag of 'Lucky' stuck and it had worked for him now and again – like the day he found the job as top hand with Broken Wheel. He loved working with cattle and he liked this place and the men O'Day em-ployed at the time, including Alamo Ames. He'd stayed on and had no real complaints – but this thing about waiting for Alamo to do the haggling over selling price stuck in his craw and took the edge off things a little for him.

Still, he was content here, mostly, and

didn't aim to kick up a fuss.

So the herd of fifteen hundred head and a few hundred steers from smaller spreads in the valley, moved out from Broken Wheel's rich canyon country just past sun-up next morning, and within an hour were trailing a dust cloud that made the washer-women and wives on the ranches spit a few words they normally would never even think, let alone utter.

The long bunched stream of cows caused a traffic jam and a major panic amongst shop-keepers with windows and displays fronting Main in town. Sheriff Marsh Kilgour hobbled out to his office door, rubbing an arthritic hip, and spat a stream of brown tobacco juice across the worn boardwalk.

'Must have a word with Morg about this,' he murmured. Though when that would be was anyone's guess.

Marsh didn't get around much any more these days.

Which didn't make him any-the-less tough, but even his past reputation as a smack-'em-down lawman wouldn't be enough to back up his words forever...

Weeks rolled by and Alamo was back with a big fistful of money from the meat-packing plants' agents, making sure Morgan savvied that Lucky Kinnane had set the scene for the final dickering long before Ames had gotten back from – wherever he had been.

He never did say where – except to Morgan, of course – and the men knew better than to ply him with liquor and hope it would loosen his tongue. Alamo was one of the old school, loyal to Morgan, and a man who kept his word.

Gradually, speculation about what might have happened to Blaine – and to Kitty O'Day, whose mighty brief visit home this time raised some querying eyebrows in town – died away and all the talk was of the sudden expansion of Broken Wheel.

Beef prices had risen and O'Day had won a contract to supply the Army at Fort Angeles, not only with beef but with horses for the cavalry as well. They were rich contracts and O'Day had squared-away with the Texas First National Bank. On the advice of Banker Hayden – not so bad a man once his mortgage payments had been cleared – had invested in more land. Broken Wheel had now become the O'Day Beef Cattle Company and Morgan's influence had spread well beyond the valley and down into Mexico and some of the eastern States as well.

He was prosperous and Lucas O'Day was not slow to take some of the credit for this prosperity.

'Pa, I think we should throw up a place in Fool's Canyon, a linecamp's not really enough, what with all them pastures just over the rise. We should have a permanent place there – I've priced some lumber, and I know we can even cut their quote by half.' He winked. 'Got some inside information that the Company's in a little trouble – and I figure we can capitalize on it...'

It was a sound idea – but it wasn't Lucas'. Alamo Ames had suggested it not long back, casually, around a campfire, but Lucas had got to hear about it while he was sharing a few drinks with Shipstead, the Land Agent.

Shipstead, expansive after a good meal and some fine brandy, let slip that the lumber company's lease had run out and they were willing to cut prices until they could find more timber to lease. And that was going to be hard, because settlers were moving in, felling their own trees, splitting their own shingles – and Broken Wheel owned most of the land.

So Lucas not only did a good deal on lumber, he quietly bought up some shares in the struggling company from men who didn't want to take the risk of losing any more money. They might make Lucas a few dollars later on, but more importantly, if the lumber company went bust, as it might if they couldn't procure a viable timber lease, then he could show Morgan his foresight in obtaining enough shares to give the O'Days a controlling interest.

A little more manipulation and the Company could easily become a holding of the O'Day Beef Cattle Company – Broken Wheel had huge tracts of timber, in the hills...

Lucas was feathering his own nest for the future and already had his father's backing in most everything he did. Morgan, with no daughter now to dote on, no adopted son to hold his interest, turned his full attention on Lucas – something Lucas had craved for most of his life. He had always felt he had played second fiddle to Kitty, and then Blaine had earned his father's respect simply because he stood up to him and was unafraid.

Yes – this was Lucas' Big Chance and he didn't aim to let it slide by.

Then, five months after Kitty had left and Blaine had vanished, an outrider brought in some strays that had wandered over from Bell's Cross B, and, off-saddling at the home corral, said casually,

'Seen a rider up on Slaughter Point today–'

'That's nothin' to write home about,' growled one of the men perched in the late afternoon sun on the corral fence watching the outrider rub down his mount. 'You can see half-a-dozen riders in a day crossin' our land over that Point.'

'Sure,' the outrider said, a Tennesseean called Curly – he was completely bald, naturally. 'But this one was wearin' buckskins – over-shirt, pants, knee-length leggin's, all buckskin.'

One of the men on the fence stiffened. 'An Injun?'

'Nah! Thought it might've been at first, but he was a whiteman, all right, had a curl-brim hat – an' – like somethin' dark on one side of his face. Maybe paint.'

'Paint could mean an Injun,' someone opined worriedly.

'Somethin' dark?' asked the original sceptic. 'What the hell's that mean?'

Curly shrugged, taking off his hat, using his sleeve to blot sweat from his glistening pate. 'I dunno, it just looked like somethin' – dark – don't matter, anyways. He turned and dropped back over the Point again.'

'Now why in hell would anyone want to climb all the way up to that Point, then turn around and go back down the way he come...? Damn big waste of energy you ask me...'

They soon dropped the subject and it wasn't even worth resurrecting over supper.

Until, just on dark, a lone horseman came into the yard and the lounging ranch hands saw that he was dressed all in buckskin – and had some kind of patch or mask on one side of his face.

Then Alamo Ames, sitting quietly on an upturned empty nail keg, stood up abruptly, watching the tall newcomer step down lithely from the saddle.

'Judas priest!' the trail boss whispered, dropping his fresh-made cigarette unlit. 'It's Blaine!'

# CHAPTER 5

## BACK TO STAY

The men started to get up and move towards the dimly seen figure, but Alamo waved them back, sauntered forward as Blaine looped the reins over the corral rail and loosened the cinch on the big, dusty sorrel.

'New hoss,' Alamo opined and Blaine looked at him slowly and the trail boss winced, seeing the scarred face, the crooked nose – and most of all, the leather patch covering the right eye. Or where it once was...

'God almighty! They – took your – eye?'

'Where's Kitty?' Blaine asked in a stiffer, colder voice than Alamo remembered.

'Gone.'

'He send her away?' At Alamo's nod, Blaine added, 'Where?'

This time Alamo said nothing, stared soberly, and after a pause, Blaine nodded slowly.

'You gave him your word, huh? Where is he?'

73

'In the house – I'll go on ahead and let him know you're...'

'Stay put.'

Blaine shouldered past the miffed trail man and Alamo took two steps after him, lifting a hand as he opened his mouth to speak, then changed his mind. 'Hell, they gotta settle it sometime...'

As Blaine entered the house, the cowboys came across from the bunkhouse, all curiosity and questions. Alamo fended them curtly.

'Dunno any more'n you – he's back. What happens next is somethin' we're just gonna have to wait and see...'

'Christ!' someone said. 'Reckon he'll kill Morg...?'

Alamo wondered about that, too.

After the first shock of seeing Blaine again wore off, Morgan O'Day made straight for the whiskey bottle in his office. The bottle neck rattled musically against the glass rim. 'You never were one to drink much, but you can help yourself if you want.'

'What'd you do with her?'

Morgan took a deep draught before he answered, wiping a slightly shaky hand across his lips. 'She's all right – safe. Out of your reach–'

Blaine waited a moment. 'She have the baby?'

'Miscarried – halfway through the third month. But she's recovered and – living a different kind of life now.'

'I hope I can take your word for that.'

Morgan bristled. 'You do what you damn well please! But I've told you and you can believe it or not.'

To give himself something to do, O'Day lit two oil lamps. It was almost full dark outside now. 'Hardesty and Rendell ain't here. I don't know where they are.'

'I can find 'em when I want 'em.'

'Your – eye. I'm truly sorry about that. It wasn't meant to be – that way.' Blaine said nothing and Morg poured another whiskey. 'You don't talk any more than you did before,' he rapped sharply but there was still no reply. 'I'd like to know what happened to you after the riverbank.'

'Thought you'd have figured it out by now.'

O'Day sipped, nodded slowly. 'I think maybe I have– Partly, anyway... Yellow Wolf's men, right?'

'Just two. They were kids when last I saw 'em – seems they've been keeping an eye on me from time to time over the years. Running Bird and Longhead.'

'Because you're Yellow Wolf's son.'

'Uh-huh– But I'm not pure blood. Whites don't have a monopoly on treating a man different because he's mixed blood. They kept watch, but on the quiet.'

That seemed to surprise Morgan, mildly. 'They must think pretty well of you, to take you in and – doctor you.'

'There's a whiteman doctor at the Agency on the Reservation. He knew my mother, Katy.' That brought Morgan's head swinging around. 'Knows about you and that raid, too.'

'Not Doc Weir? He still around?'

'Made a career out of working with the tribes. He set my nose, slung my jaw in a damn leather sling for over a month while the bones healed. Fed me liquid mush through a reed... Couldn't save my eye, though he tried. Clem Hardesty turned it to mush with his boot heel.'

Morgan looked uncomfortable, drained his glass and refilled it after a slight hesitation.

'Like I said, it wasn't meant to...'

'I heard you the first time.'

Morg turned slowly, eyes burning. 'You

sayin' you don't believe me?' But he sounded nervous, unsure...

Blaine didn't answer and saw the man stiffen and just as Morgan was about to blow, said, 'I didn't come here to kill you – I'll get Hardesty and Rendell sometime, but there's no hurry. They're dead mean already – just don't know it.'

Frowning, O'Day asked, 'Why did you come back then?'

'To square with you.'

'You just said...'

'I said I didn't come back to kill you – and I didn't. But I've got a lot more than a bad beating to square with you, Morg.'

O'Day didn't like the atmosphere now. There was a coldness in this room, his *sanctum*, alive with memories in the shape of tin-types and faded post cards, old tattered letters locked away in carved-wood boxes. Here had always been a kind of retreat where he could come to and let the good memories soothe him from the worries of the present, a warm, comfortable place.

But not with this one-eyed breed standing here, gun-hung, solid as a statue, menacing without even trying.

'I dunno what the hell you're talkin' about – I treated you well enough. You couldn't

expect the same as I gave Lucas or Kitty–'
He stumbled over the word and Blaine
knew he had disowned her.

'You treated me well enough,' Blaine
broke in and puzzlement swept over the
rancher's face like a tide coming in at the
sea shore. 'Gave me a life, educated me a
little, fed me, clothed me, called a sawbones
when I needed one, taught me about cows–'

'Then, what...?'

'Morg – *that's* what I owe you. All those
things. You told me yourself you'd spent a
lot of money rearing me, keeping your word
to my mother. You said I'd have to pay you
back for those things...'

'That – that was just talk. I was riled
a'plenty and...'

'I aim to square my obligations to you,
Morgan. You mentioned you'd put me to
work, in effect, take the money out of my
hide. Well, I'm agreeable to that. Where do
you want me to start? Back in my old
position, *segundo* to Lucas? Something
else...?'

The air was hissing from Morgan's large
nostrils now and his eyes were narrowed.
*Hell, what had he raised here...? This was totally
unexpected and he wasn't sure how to handle
it...* Then the old tough cattleman asserted

his hard nature once again, feeling confidence surging through him as he did so.

'All right! You think I'm loco enough to say "no" to an offer like that?' He shook his silver head vigorously. 'No, sir! It's just what I want – you'll work to pay me back for what it's cost me to raise you. You'll have your keep and a little *dinero* – very little! But I'll take it out of your hide until I say "stop" – you get that? *I'm* the one to say "'nough", call it quits. Until then, you do as I say...'

He stopped dead as Blaine shook his head. 'No, you can call it quits when you're satisfied, but as for me doing everything you say – *I'll* be the one to judge that.'

'Now, listen here...!'

'Workwise, OK, I'll follow orders. But that's where it stops, Morg. Leave my personal life alone. You don't boss me around like the kid with a hole in his pants that I was when I first came here. I'm Blaine now: Black Dog to the Comanche, if it's of any interest to you. I'll work and work hard, and do as good a job as I can – but that'll be your only interest in me.'

Morg blazed in the old style, shaking a thick finger across his desk. 'You don't talk to me like that!'

Blaine put on his hat and turned to the

79

door, stumbling into a chair on his right side. He smothered a curse but Morg heard and his seamed face softened some.

'One eye – must make it – pretty tough, huh?'

'Not as good as two,' Blaine admitted. 'You want me to move out of my old room...?'

The rancher nodded, sensing he could have the final victory here. 'Yeah, you're on a different footin' here now, just another hired hand. There'll be room in the bunkhouse.'

Blaine nodded and went out. Morgan O'Day poured another glass of whiskey and held it up to the light. His hand was still shaking slightly.

'Well – here's to you, Morgan Patrick O'Day. When that man walked through that door I didn't expect to still be able to do this–' He shuddered as the whiskey hit the back of his throat and added huskily, 'or anythin' else!'

Alamo Ames paused as he buckled the leather chest-piece on his horse, ready for brush-popping mavericks high up in the sawtooths. He watched Blaine fumble a little getting the strap ends through the buckles as he fixed the leather to his sorrel.

'One eye make a big difference?'

80

'Some. Had to learn to shoot a rifle all over again.'

The trail boss blinked. 'How come?'

'You can't shoot a rifle up to your right shoulder with only your left eye to sight with – Can't shoot accurately, nor even fast. Got to sight straight down the barrel, so I had to learn to use the rifle with my left hand.'

Alamo grunted, scratching his head. 'Six gun?'

'That's OK – can still use my right hand and just point. Maybe not as good as before, but it works.'

'No wonder you were so long with the Injuns...'

Blaine tested the buckles on the chest-piece and, satisfied, swung up into the saddle. It wasn't done as smoothly before he lost the eye, Alamo noticed.

Morgan had decided to have Blaine work with Alamo, rounding-up and branding mavericks, and other cattle considered prime enough for the trail drives. The rancher decided he would feel easier if Blaine was away from Broken Wheel much of the time. Maybe it was Morg's conscience – he sure wouldn't admit to himself that it might be uneasiness, still not certain about Blaine's intentions.

The entire valley was stunned when they heard that Blaine was back, not with a smoking gun in his hand, but volunteering to work off what he figured he owed Morgan O'Day. It won Blaine a lot more admiration that he knew, even from those who, previously, had figured O'Day was out of his mind, taking on the raising of a half-breed and expecting some good to come of it...

Lucas was possibly the only one who didn't see anything good in Blaine's return. He tried to sway Morgan whenever the chance occurred.

'He's just waiting, Pa! Waiting for his chance – then he's gonna bust us good!'

'Us? You think he'd spend any energy this way to square with *you?* Lord knows he's had plenty to put up with from you over the years and he's whaled the tar out of you from time to time – and I had to stick up for my son, of course, and punish him. But that was enough for someone like Blaine, giving you a black eye or a bloody nose – he don't think you're worth much more'n that.'

That hurt Lucas and he flushed deeply. 'How about you? You figure that's all I'm worth? A scuffle in the dust ten years ago...?'

Morgan sighed. 'I'm sayin' that's the way

Blaine sees it – forget him. You just keep managin' Broken Wheel the way you're going – you're doin' a good job.'

Lucas preened at those rare words of praise from his father. 'Yeah, well, like you say, Blaine's just another hired hand now...'

'Alamo'll take care of him. He needs experience in trail drivin'.'

Lucas frowned.

'You make that sound like he's got some sort of –future here.'

Morg scowled, but there was a slightest suggestion of a crooked smile there, too. 'How long you think it's gonna be before I holler "quits"? You think Blaine's gonna get this all squared away in six months – even a year?'

Lucas smiled slowly then: he knew the Old Man was as sharp as ever.

He was going to keep that breed working his butt off until he dropped – then kick him to his feet and work him some more...

Alamo and Blaine hadn't had a lot to do with each other over the years, but they always got along pretty well. Blaine had helped out with the trail drives occasionally but mostly he had been kept on ranch chores – Lucas giving him those he didn't want to do himself in the early days, before he managed to talk his father around into letting him take care of the books.

As the days of rounding-up the mavericks passed and they spent time together, camped out in the hills and canyons, Alamo and Blaine formed a closer bond. The trail boss knew he could never break through the 'breed's reserve but they had short conversations on general topics now, something Alamo had never been able to initiate previously.

'You think about Kitty a lot, don't you?'

Alamo had decided that Blaine would never ask him about the girl, respected him too much to expect him to break his word to Morgan.

'You said she's all right – I'm taking you at your word.'

'Good – because she'll be fine where she is. It was her choice in the end. I think maybe Morgan had calmed down some and might've taken her back – sort of – but when *she* decided what she wanted to do, he disowned her – says he don't have a daughter.'

'Must be hard on her – she thought a lot of her father.'

'Only natural: her mother died when she was very young, only months old. Morg's the only real parent she ever knew – Lucas was different. He could remember his mother a little–'

Blaine tossed his coffee dregs into the fire abruptly. 'Guess I'll turn in – I'm tired. You're a slave-driver, Alamo.'

'Hell, I can give you nigh on twenty years and I ain't tired – well, not *real* tired.'

'Good, then I'll leave you to check the mounts and the cattle pens.'

As Blaine moved away, Alamo said, 'Hey! You better be careful, you almost smiled then!'

But neither man was smiling a couple of hours later when the cattle they had gathered and penned-up in a gulch came bawling and snorting and horn-swinging through the camp in all-out stampede.

Above the noise and the thunder, both Alamo and Blaine heard the rap of gun shots, driving the killer herd on.

# CHAPTER 6

## LONG VENGEANCE

They grabbed their horses, dragging them by sheer force up the slope as the first of the steers came bawling and slobbering into the camp area. Blaine had snatched his rifle and his six gun was thrust into his belt. Alamo had his Colt but had fumbled his rifle and lost it in the hurry to get his mount out of the way of the thundering herd.

Blaine swung aboard the sorrel, wrenching aside as sharp-tipped horns raked down the mount's hide. It whinnied and reared and lunged aside, bleeding but not, apparently, seriously hurt.

Blaine swung the rifle across his body and down, firing into the lunging, mindless steer, the bullet smashing in behind the ear. The bovine animal went down as if something had cut the legs from under it, the big red-and-white blotched body somersaulting, hoofs flailing in a final throe. Blaine's horse swung aside and he spun the rifle around the trigger guard, fired into a second beast, saw dust spurt from its back. It staggered but didn't go down. Alamo's six gun was banging and as Blaine fought his mount around – it wanted only to escape this writhing crush of horned devil-beasts – he glimpsed a rider on the slope above. Just a dark shape, but the man was throwing down at the trail boss with his rifle.

The half-breed gripped the writhing sorrel hard, feeling the muscles ridging and snaking under his thighs. It was a wild seat from which to draw a bead, but Blaine remembered in time he no longer had a right eye, switched the rifle butt to his left shoulder, sighted and triggered, levered and triggered again.

He thought he hit the man's horse rather than the killer himself, saw the animal go down head first and then the shadowed body sailing through the air. The man hit some brush and it was thick enough and springy enough to throw him on to the slope. Dazed, but still holding his rifle and some yards above the stampeding stream, he spread his boots and drew another bead on Alamo who was sitting astride his quivering mount, try-ing to reload with fumbling fingers.

Blaine rowelled savagely, letting the sorrel

know who was in charge here, and it stopped an upslope lunge, speared forward in the direction Blaine wanted it to go. The killer must have heard it snorting coming in, or maybe the drum of shod hoofs on the hard ground, for he began to swing around, rifle lifting to meet the new threat. He was a tad slow and the sorrel smashed into him and drove him down to the slope. He lost the rifle, rolled violently but came up to one knee, Colt in his right hand, left chopping across, ready to fan the hammer.

Blaine's bullet took him between the eyes, snapping his head back as if he had run into an unseen tree branch. The man's feet left the ground and the horse struck him again, stumbling.

As the breed brought the mount around, steadying it, he coughed in the choking dust, saw the tail end of the herd coming over the rise. Two more riders were shooting into the sky, spotted him and Alamo, and changed their aim. The two Broken Wheel men emptied their guns and one man slid sideways and almost fell out of the saddle, but regained balance at the last moment and dropped back into the darkness.

The other man could be heard galloping away fast. Alamo skidded his mount up alongside Blaine, panting. 'They weren't Injuns!'

Blaine said nothing, spurred the sorrel over the rise where the other two killers had disappeared, but there was nothing to see. He rode on, crouching low, thumbing fresh loads into his rifle. Then up ahead an orange dagger stabbed the darkness and he felt the air-whip of a slug passing his face. He dropped his spare shells and the rifle, too, lunged for it and spilled from the saddle. By the time he had stopped rolling and the horse had come to a halt some yards away, the killers were gone.

Alamo rode up. 'Sons of bitches! They wanted us bad! Or you, leastways. They didn't have to stop and try to nail you when they had such a good lead. This was personal!'

Breathing hard, Blaine dusted himself down, went to the quivering sorrel and examined the horn wound as well he could. It was deep enough to hurt and bleed, but shallow enough not to require any urgent treatment.

'Camp's a damn mess,' Alamo allowed but didn't expect a reply: he had learned that Blaine wasn't a man to either state the obvious or acknowledge a man who did. 'Well, there goes three days work and the cows'll be scattered to hell and gone by mornin'.'

'I got one of 'em – up the slope yonder.'

They walked their horses across to where the dead man lay, face shattered by the bullet, body mangled by the sorrel's hoofs. Blaine figured the others were long gone and struck a vesta but cupped a hand around the flame.

'Know him?'

Alamo craned forward, studying the dead man. 'Hard to tell – looks kinda familiar, though. I think it's Candy Starke. Worked a season for Broken Wheel while you were away. Got caught goin' through the other men's warbags... After the crew got through with him, they tied him to a mule and turned him loose up at the far end of Fool's Canyon. Ain't heard of nor seen him since.'

'Then he'd have no love for Broken Wheel?'

'Not Candy – but, somethin' else – he was a friend of Hardesty and Rendell.'

Blaine nodded slowly. 'We might's well turn in again– Can't do anything about the steers tonight and we'll need daylight to study the tracks.'

The herd was scattered far and wide, some

of the mavericks, now they had calmed down after the panic of stampede, searching out their old haunts, deep in the most in-accessible scrub.

'This's gonna put us behind,' Alamo opined, face grim. 'We'll have to call up a couple of extra hands to help with the round-up. That won't make Morgan happy!'

'Can you get along without me?'

Alamo's eyebrows were arching in surprise before he had turned completely around. 'Where you goin'?'

'Took a look at the tracks on the rise – where I winged one before he got away and his pard took that potshot at me. I reckon Hardesty and Rendell are still forking the same broncs they rode before they beat on me.'

Alamo frowned. 'You can remember those tracks?'

'Sure – Clem's black always threw its right forefoot slightly out to one side, making the track lopsided – Clint had the little grey with the dainty hoofs, making a mark almost like a large deer instead of a hoss.'

Alamo Ames scratched his head. 'You've got a deal of Indian blood workin' in you, all right, Blaine! But I guess you could be right – Curly saw 'em at the water tanks along the

91

railroad a few weeks back and sure enough, they were still forkin' the same broncs they had when they rode for Broken Wheel.'

Blaine was already mounted. 'I'll see if I can catch up with them.'

'Wait! They'll be long gone by now and we need to get them steers penned again! They gotta go in with the main herd and there ain't a lot of time to spare before we start headin' 'em-up and movin' out to railhead...'

'I'll be back as quick as I can.'

'Dammit, Blaine! I'm s'posed to be in charge here!'

'You are, Alamo– You are. You're the trail boss.'

'Well, then why the hell is it when I tell you I want you to do somethin, you do what *you* want?'

Blaine was already swinging the sorrel away. 'Must've hit my head when I fell last night – can't hardly hear... *Adios*, Alamo.'

Ames started to yell, whipping off his hat and throwing it on the ground, but he didn't persevere as Blaine rode upslope towards the ridge. *What was the use?*

Blaine's vengeance had been a long time coming – and he might as well get it over and done with before the trail drive started.

It never occurred to Alamo for a moment

that Blaine might not return from his vengeance trail.

The trail was easy to follow: after all, the fugitives had been intent only on escape, and in the dark at that.

Still, Blaine rode with his fully-loaded rifle out, butt resting on his left thigh, swinging his head from side to side. Having only one eye was more of a handicap than just not being able to see with binocular vision. Swinging the head from one side to the other so as to cover all country brought on a vague dizziness, simply with the motion. It wasn't enough to make him want to grip the saddle harder, but it did feel as if he wasn't quite in full control of his body.

After he cleared the ridge and picked his way down into a wide canyon with a stream flowing across the sandy floor, the tracks were a little more difficult to find. But he saw the blood spots and the piece of bloody rag where the wounded man had tried to give his injury some attention. Or, maybe even his pard had done it for him, though Blaine, knowing both men, figured this was unlikely. In the world of Hardesty and Rendell, it was Number One first, last and always...

He had no plan, simply aiming to track these men down now he had started. He had been content to wait a while longer for it was already six months since they had beat him up and taken his eye. But making that move against him and Alamo last night – well, that was a declaration of war as far as Blaine was concerned.

This time he would end it – and he aimed to ride away the victor.

He trailed the men coldly and relentlessly, clear through the canyon and into some draws where they had doubled-back and swung off at a southern tangent, trying to cover their tracks all the way. But though he had been only four years old when Morgan had taken him from the Comanche, he had already had a basic knowledge of tracking small animals. During his months of recovery just recently, Running Bird had shown him how to follow man tracks, and the poor covering-up methods that white men used. He had shown Blaine something of an Indian's way of covering tracks and Blaine was astounded: no wonder Alamo and his men had found nothing at the riverbank when Running Bird and Long Head had whisked him away with his injuries.

But although he soon uncovered the trail

Hardesty and Rendell had tried to hide, he didn't realise how close behind the men he was. Likely the injured man had slowed them down and he wondered at this, having expected the unharmed one would have ridden on and left the other to his fate. He knew now it was Rendell who was wounded, having found, half-buried, a torn, blood-stained neckerchief that he recognized: it was heavily soiled with sweat and dirt and he recalled Clint Rendell had worn that same neckerchief for weeks at a time before rinsing it perfunctorily in a creek's murky water. Besides, the man's horse had left meandering tracks as if the rider wasn't in full control of the reins.

But he was closer than he knew.

The rifles blasted from the high rocks. One bullet geysered gravel a yard in front of the swerving sorrel. The other tugged at his buckskin shirt where it hung in a loose fold across his chest.

Naturally, they had blind-sided him, shooting from his right.

Blaine was going out of the saddle, kicking boots free of the stirrups, holding his rifle high as he tipped his body to the left. He kicked the horse with a boot as he fell and it whickered, lurched, then ran off, instinctively hunting cover in the lower clump of boulders.

Blaine rolled swiftly towards a line of broken rocks, hearing the dull rifle shots as his body crunched across the gravel, his boots scrabbling wildly, seeking purchase so as to thrust him into shelter. Before he made it, two bullets flung rock chips against his hat and he ducked his head instinctively, squirmed in and sprawled as flat as possible.

Breathing hard, dust biting at his nostrils, he turned his face with his good eye uppermost, searching for the gunsmoke. It hung in a pall in the still air. If he had been pursuing his quarry in open country the breeze would have whipped it away or shredded it. This way, the grey-white powdersmoke cloud pinpointed the bushwhackers' hiding place.

He slid the rifle from under his body, snugged the butt into his left shoulder and sighted just below the smoke, seeing now the gap between the big rocks up there.

His finger tightened on the trigger as he laid his sights on that gap – then he slacked-off, moved the barrel several inches and lower. He fired three fast shots into rocks that were six feet below and three feet to the side of the killers' hiding place. *That would give them confidence and maybe make them careless –*

*thinking he didn't know yet where they were.*

He fired several more shots, well away from the actual gap where Hardesty and Rendell were. As he reloaded from his bullet belt, they raked his shelter and he heard someone laugh.

'We got you pinned, Blaine!' That was Hardesty.

Blaine didn't make any reply, shifted his aim, but made it a little closer this time. They would still figure he was shooting blind. *The sons of bitches were half-right! But they were about to pay for that!*

He waited a few minutes and sure enough he saw the movement up there, Hardesty still over-confident. There was the smear of the man's shadow at first and then the dull colour of a sweaty checked shirt, the glint of the rifle barrel.

Blaine's Winchester snapped to his shoulder and blazed two fast shots. There was a startled scream, the clatter of a falling weapon as it tumbled down into the rocks below. Hardesty had fallen back, or been blown back out of the gap. There was no answering shot from Rendell: maybe he was too badly hurt to put up much of a fight.

Whatever the reason, it was all over now.

Blaine jumped up, ran left, then zigzagged

in close under the high boulders where any-one above would have to half-stand and crane outwards, exposing their upper body, to see a man below. Swivelling his head for handholds, Blaine climbed swiftly, fell twice but with minimum noise. There was one shot from above but he heard the bullet ricochet from his previous hiding place: they hadn't seen him leave it and start moving up to-wards them. Might only be Rendell alive by now. He wasn't sure where he had shot Har-desty.

But he soon found out, when he hauled himself up and over a rock that looked like a decapitated boiled egg, found footing on the broken, slightly tilted surface, and swung his rifle around to cover the two men sprawled amongst the rocks below.

Rendell had been hit in the thigh, it seemed, one leg held stiff and straight, bloody rags roughly tied over the wound. Clem Hardesty was lying in a half-sitting position, blood pouring from a bullet gouge across his face, and more blood pumping out of a chest wound.

Both men raised pain-filled and now fear-glazed eyes as Blaine cocked his rifle.

'Time to pay the fiddler, boys.'

The Winchester blasted and Rendell

jarred and screamed as a bullet smashed his good knee and left him huddled and whimpering against his rock.

The Winchester crashed again and Hardesty jerked and cried out as a bullet shattered his right hip.

Blaine climbed down carefully and stood over the sobbing, bloody men. He set his rifle on a rock at his head level, picked up the men's guns and tossed them away to clatter amongst the boulders.

Then he squatted between the two wounded, terrified killers, looking from one to the other as he drew his hunting blade from its fringed sheath.

'Who's first?' he asked grimly.

## CHAPTER 7

### IN OLD MONTERREY

Morgan O'Day stepped out on to the porch, watching the scene down by the corrals. He sucked on a new cherrywood pipe and would be glad when the bowl had burned-in to his satisfaction.

Through the cloud of aromatic smoke he puffed, he saw Alamo talking animatedly with Lucas who had happened to be down at the corrals, tallying the remuda so the wrangler could decide which mounts would go with the trail herd.

Morgan had noticed from his office that Lucas seemed agitated and he had known Alamo long enough to recognize rising anger in the trail boss by the set of his body. O'Day spat and called for Lucas and Alamo to come up to the porch.

'Trouble?' he asked as Alamo Ames stomped into the shade followed more slowly by Lucas, who looked deep in thought, carrying his ever-present notepads.

'Some high-riders busted the mavericks last night, stampeded 'em through the camp – Blaine's gone after 'em so I need a couple men to help me roundup the steers.'

'Blaine oughta had more sense,' Lucas snapped, quick to put another black mark against the breed.

Alamo said quietly, 'It was Hardesty and Rendell.'

'Now there's a pair,' allowed Morgan, his face tight. 'You shoulda stopped Blaine – I oughta send someone after him.' It was just talk and he knew the others knew it: Blaine would do as he pleased, specially with a sighting of the men who had almost killed him. 'But we've just had word that the meat-packing houses won't send their agents down to our railhead from now on.'

Lucas snapped his head up. 'Damn! I knew it! They were hinting at it last time, sayin' it was too far to come, just for our longhorns. They don't think much of 'em.'

'Longhorn beefs good enough for the Army,' bristled Morgan. 'But, it's the distance and our railhead only bein' on a spur-track: facilities are pretty rough. The new railhead at San Antone's opened, links directly with the big tracks to the Gulf Coast. They'll meet us there from now on.'

'They want us to drive to *San Antone!*' asked Lucas, outraged. 'Hell's teeth, that's gonna cost a pretty penny...'

'Which'll be reflected in our asking price.'

'Sure – but will they pay our price?'

'Reckon so – we'll take bigger herds, drive just once a year. It'll work out in the end.'

Alamo shrugged. 'Ten thousand or thirty thousand won't make no difference to me long as I have enough men.'

'You will...'

Lucas suddenly snapped his fingers. 'Listen, Pa – we can boost our quality and practically guarantee top dollar.'

'You can't do that overnight, boy!'

Lucas flushed – *when the hell was the Old Man going to quit calling him 'boy'? Damnit, he was pushing thirty and still he...*

Aloud he said, 'We're pushin' it some to fill those Army contracts, Pa.'

'Which is why I sent Alamo after them mavericks.'

'Yeah, well, when I was in town seeing Calvin Eastbrook about the new timber leases, he told me that Don Miguel Santiago was selling his place down at San Nicolas.'

Morgan frowned. 'That's near Monterrey, ain't it?'

Alamo looked at his boss but Lucas went on quickly.

'Yeah, Pa – Calvin heard on the quiet the old *hidalgo* is dyin' and aimed to spread his *rancho* amongst his family, but none of 'em are much interested in the workin' side of things: all they want is cold hard cash. So to spite 'em, he's sellin' up at bargain prices... We could pick us up some prime breeding stock, Pa, as well as some to sell.'

Alamo could see Morgan was almost persuaded, but, as he expected, the rancher said, 'Long way down to Monterrey – or San Nicolas which is almost as far. Can't spare the men for the drive back.'

Lucas smiled, winking at Alamo. 'A good man could dicker so that old Miguel provides the *vaqueros* to get 'em back to the Border... We can let you know when we're there and half-a-dozen men'd be enough to drive 'em back here, take just a day or two...'

'You ain't goin',' Morg said flatly and Lucas' face fell.

'Aw, Pa, it's my idea and I'd sure like to do some horse-trading with that old *ranchero!* After all the sneaky damn tricks he's pulled on us Texas ranchers in general, over the years...'

'Alamo can handle it – he's good at buyin' cows, better even than sellin' 'em.' He flicked his hard old eyes to the trail boss. 'You could do it, couldn't you?'

Lucas frowned as Alamo nodded slowly. There was something that passed between his father and the grizzled trail boss ... he had no idea what it was, but there was *something* there and it only made Lucas feel more put-out. But he knew once Morgan had made up his mind – well, that was that.

'All right – I'll contact the agent down in San Nicolas and tell him Alamo's on his way...You'll need to take a couple men with you.'

'Reckon I'll be able to talk Don Miguel into lendin' us a few *vaqueros* for the drive back to the Border...'

Lucas' frown deepened as Morgan shot Alamo a quick, piercing look. 'You reckon you're that good?'

The trail boss nodded. 'But just in case Don Miguel won't give us any trail hands, maybe Blaine could call in a bunch of his cousins or whatever from the Reservation – that way, you won't have to bother about sendin' down anyone from here, Morg, and leave you short-handed.'

'Injuns!' exclaimed Lucas. 'Not working our prime beeves, thanks all the same!'

'I'll be there and Blaine knows how to handle 'em.'

'He ought to! But I don't like this, Pa. Not Injuns!'

'No, Blaine doesn't go – you oughta have more sense than to suggest it, Alamo...' Morg looked mighty angry.

Lucas was quick to side with his father. 'None of us can trust that damn breed...'

'You go send your wire to the cattle agent while Alamo and me fix this between us...' growled Morgan.

*That* didn't make Lucas feel any more wanted, or even that his father was grateful for his suggestion that would save the ranch money and, in effect, bring in more profit when the herd reached the new rail-head at San Antonio.

*Even after all that had happened, the Old Man still seemed to be favouring that damn 'breed!*

And Lucas decided he'd just about had a bellyful.

Alamo left two men gathering up the scattered mavericks and went looking for Blaine. The man's trail was easy enough to follow. He hadn't been trying to hide his tracks – had no reason to – and Alamo had no trouble following him up and over the ridge, through Big Sandy canyon and into the eroded gulch country beyond.

There was no breeze here, surrounded as it was by high buttes and walls of large boulders, and Alamo, a man born and bred to the wilderness and who had spent his life there, smelled the gunsmoke still hovering in the air. New scars on the rocks showed him where bullets had struck and he saw the loose rocks and fresh, dark patches of earth where Blaine's boots had found footholds as he climbed up to the boulders above.

He took his rifle with him and climbed

quietly, wary, not taking it for granted that Blaine had subdued those two murdering hardcases. He would have expected him to, but a man could never tell and it paid to take precautions.

There were no sounds from above but he smelled tobacco smoke – and something else. Like when tracking a deer that had been shot and you were closing in on where it lay, either bleeding to death or simply playing possum.

It was the stench of blood. And death.

'God almighty!'

Alamo breathed the words reverently, feeling his stomach lurch, and his hands gripped the rifle convulsively as he looked down on the scene below him.

Blaine was sitting with his back to a boulder, smoking, knees drawn up, forearms resting on them, head down. If he heard Alamo – and he must have – he didn't look up. His hands were red.

Ames stared at the dead men lying in a welter of blood that had splashed on some of the rocks like spilled paint. He swallowed, saw the sun glint redly from a discarded hunting knife near Hardesty's raw face. It looked as if he had been skinned alive...

Both he and Clint Rendell had been

scalped and there were other mutilations that Alamo didn't care to dwell on.

Then he saw that Blaine was staring at him as he drew on his cigarette, dark face blank – but Alamo thought he saw a little more peace in that single bleak grey-green eye. He thumbed back his hat.

'Well, I said a little while back that you sure had a deal of Injun blood workin' in you – I don't blame you, but – well...' *To hell with Morgan! He couldn't leave Blaine here with this mess... If Marsh Kilgour got wind of it, no telling what he might do to Blaine...* 'We best bury these fellers and then you and me are headin' down to Mexico. You ask me, it's the best place for you right now...'

Blaine finished his cigarette and stood, brushing dust off his trousers.

'I'll get something to dig with,' was all he said.

San Nicolas was a well-established Spanish town and Don Miguel's large holdings were ten miles southeast, closer to Monterrey than San Nicolas. The *rancho* was typical of that part of the country, large white *hacienda* and adobe outbuildings, stables and corrals and a couple of windmills, an unusual innovation for a Mexican ranch.

It didn't take Blaine long to figure that Alamo Ames knew Don Miguel, although he could never recall the man mentioning it.

'Worked for him long ago,' Alamo told Blaine, 'before I went to Morgan's – he kind of took care of me after my folks was wiped out in a wagon train to the north by bandits and renegade Apaches. It was part of the country a *hidalgo* like him was expected to protect – a bit like the old feudal times – and he felt he'd let the folk down. Anyway, we got along well enough and then one day I followed a Mexican gal who was governess to his children back to the States where she had another job.'

He paused and Blaine waited, patient as usual, reading Alamo correctly in thinking the man was hesitant to explain any more. But the trail boss said, with a rush of words, 'We married – but she was trampled by a runaway hoss and crippled. Afterwards, she figured she was a burden to me and one night–' He shook his head at the black memory clouding his mind. 'I dunno where she got the poison, but–'

He looked steadily at Blaine who nodded gently, but made no other sign that he understood.

'Anyway – I reckon I can do a good deal

with Don Miguel. We'd parted friends.'

The old *ranchero* was in a great deal of pain from whatever ailment was killing him and he spoke in husky Spanish, gripping Alamo's hand. The trail boss flicked his eyes at Blaine who took the hint and waited outside in the cool shade of a long tiled patio, sipping lemonade, lime and *tequila* that a servant brought him. It was a mighty satisfying drink for hot weather.

When Alamo emerged from Don Miguel's quarters he was long-faced. 'Too bad – shame to lose a man like that. He's done plenty for this country but seems his family's let him down – want the bright lights, such as they are, plenty of partyin' and the high life. Cash is all they want from him so the only way he can get back at 'em now is to sell as cheap as possible.'

'Could change his will.'

'Too late – the family's got the lawyer in their pockets. He's blockin' the Don every whichway.'

Blaine nodded: the old Don had been smart enough anyway. 'You do a deal for Morg?'

'Yeah – we got five hundred prime beeves to get back to Broken Wheel. Don Miguel will supply riders to help us all the way – I'd thought maybe we could call in some of your Injun friends but this way we won't need 'em.'

Blaine nodded, making no comment.

'One favour the Don asks, though – and it'll have to be you to do it, Blaine.'

This surprised the breed.

'Yeah, there's this kind of orphanage or sanctuary just outside Monterrey. Don Miguel has helped them some over the years. He's got half-a-dozen Jersey milkers he thinks they can use – called Mission *Seguridad,* by the way. Some Sisters from the big Mission run it.'

'Nuns?'

'No-ooo – I dunno. Maybe novices... Anyway, you're elected to drive the Jerseys up there. You can take one of Don Miguel's men or *muchachos* along...'

'Never driven milkers before.'

'They're docile. Won't give you no trouble – he wants you to give one of the Fathers a note, too. Think he's gonna ask that one of 'em stays down here on the *rancho* with him till he – passes away. Be sure of the Last Rites I guess.'

The *muchacho*'s name was Pancho and he spoke no American. His Spanish was too rapid for Blaine. So while the kid ran around with his stick, whacking the cows if they strayed too far or stopped too long, browsing on the scanty grass, Blaine let his sorrel make its own pace and he smoked as they moved along lazily through the early afternoon.

The orphanage was set behind adobe walls and he could see the small tower of a chapel above, but had to wait until they were inside to see the buildings. There were several, mostly adobe, though a long one which he figured for a dormitory, was clapboard with a thatched roof. All seemed in good repair and he noticed several women working with bunches of children who all wore flour-sack, dress-like garments, whether boy or girl. The latter were distinguishable by their longer hair, although several had it cropped – no doubt as part of a treatment for head lice.

One of the women came across as Pancho, obviously having been here before, drove the Jerseys towards a small corral. A bunch of yelling, excited children ran on ahead and lowered the rails for him.

'*Señor?*' queried the woman in nun-like garments and Blaine said,

'A gift from Don Miguel Santiago – I was told to ask for Sister Maria de Gracia.'

The woman who faced him was in her fifties, her serene face remarkably free of wrinkles, though the brown blotches on the backs of her hands gave some indication of her age. Her eyes were very blue and they squinted a little as she turned her face towards him enough so that the shadow of her stiff headpiece moved and allowed sun glare to strike her. *'Norteamericano?'*

Blaine nodded. 'From Texas, ma'am.'

Her expression didn't change. 'I am Sister Angelica, in charge here – I will write Don Miguel a note of thanks. Sister Maria de Gracia will join you.' She gestured to a small patio, shaded by an umbrella-like shelter of thatch on a long pole beneath which was a round table and some chairs. 'She will bring you refreshment.'

'Obliged.' Blaine made his way there, feeling a little awkward. He didn't really need to see this Sister de Gracia. *What the hell kind of name was that anyway? Sister of Thanks?* Now the cows had been delivered and he had spoken with the nun in charge, all he had to do was hand over the note to Father Gabriel and then he could go. This place made him feel – well, kind of awkward. Or was it that these laughing kids reminded him of the little Indian children who had helped him get used to walking again, steering him safely past obstacles he could no longer see on his right side... *Maybe he should have done something for them before he left to pay his debts – both to Morgan and Hardesty and Rendell... Well, he could set that right when he got back...*

But right now he could do with a long, cool drink – though he figured there would be no *tequila* in the lemonade here.

He was smoking, half turned away from the main adobe building, watching Pancho playing with the kids near the corrals, when he heard the small clatter of glasses and he turned slowly.

A young woman in a habit like Sister Angelica's, except the headpiece was no more than a scarf draped over her hair, was setting down a bamboo tray with glasses and a terracotta jug on it.

'You wished to see me, *señor?*'

As she spoke quietly in perfect English she picked up the jug and poured some clear, brownish liquid into the glasses. 'I do not know Don Miguel personally so I am at a loss as to why he told you to ask for me... I am, of course Sister Maria de Gracia.'

*It was Alamo who had told him to ask for this woman, not Don Miguel – and now he knew why...*

He stood up quickly and she turned her face towards him and he saw her properly for the first time.

'Thought I recognized that voice – Been a long time, Kitty... A *long* time.'

The jug fell and shattered on the stone flags, cool liquid splashing over Blaine's boots – washing away the last traces of Hardesty's blood.

# CHAPTER 8

## HOWDY AND ADIOS

She insisted on clearing away the mess first and he knew she was using the time to get her thoughts in order. He didn't push her, though his own heart had an unfamiliar racy feeling to it and his stomach seemed knotted.

Finally, she came back, the scarf removed from her hair now and he noted it was shorter than he remembered. But she looked somehow older – no, more mature, might be the better way of putting it. He couldn't tell if she had gained or lost weight under that loose habit but she seemed healthy enough, deeply tanned, and several children ran over, crawled up into her lap and threw their thin arms about her neck. She spoke to each in gentle Spanish, set them down and told the third one to tell the others that they should play with Sister Mercia while she entertained her guest.

Then she sipped from her glass, looking at Blaine over the rim.

'You've suffered since I last saw you, Blaine.'

'Some.'

'Was it – Hardesty and Rendell?' He met and held her gaze and she sighed. 'I know it was! Dad was raging and I knew he would sick them on to you... I'm sorry.'

'No need.'

'No *need*! Heavens, you've lost an eye!'

'And you lost your baby.'

She tensed but only slightly. 'I'm glad you know and that I won't have to explain – it – it was horrible. I – didn't handle it very well, but Sister Angelica and the others helped me, guided me...'

'You look content.'

'I – am, mostly, Blaine – I love working here with the children. I'm not a nun, but a kind of *unofficial* mission helper, I suppose.'

'Pay well?'

And the remark surprised her: Blaine wasn't really known for his attempts at humour. But she smiled widely. 'Yes – it pays very well. Though I don't earn a dime.'

'I understand.' And she knew he did: he was quick to savvy such things and it was why she had told him the details of how she had become pregnant. 'I – missed you.'

'Yes – I've missed you, too, Blaine. But didn't Alamo tell you where I was...? I mean, he brought me here in the first place...'

'He gave his word to Morgan he'd never tell me.'

She smiled slowly. 'So he had you drive some milking cows up here from Don Miguel's!'

'Alamo's a man of his word, follows his own code.'

'Just like you – does this mean you've gone back to working for my father?'

'Yes.'

She waited, then spread her hands. 'And...? Surely *that* requires some explanation.'

He shrugged. 'Morgan feels I owe him too much to let me go.'

'I don't understand...?'

'He reared me – along with you and Lucas. Took care of me for more'n twenty years. He outlayed heaps on me.'

Kitty was shocked. 'You're not serious! He – he surely wouldn't be that – petty!' She

116

stood, unable to contain herself, took a turn around the patio, came back and stood beside his chair. 'Oh! My father's – one of a kind! And I'm being as liberal as I can when saying that! But – you. You didn't have to do this... Oh! I'm *wrong*. Of course, you *did*, didn't you? You wouldn't be Blaine if you turned away from him and just rode out.'

Blaine drained his glass. 'I like to pay my debts.'

She shook her head as she slowly took her seat again. Her hand slid across the table and lay across his.

'He'll keep you working for him for years – and not pay you a cent in real money.'

'He's already spent a small fortune on me.'

'Oh, you exasperate me, Blaine! He spent more on Lucas and me – yes, we're his blood-kin but he *adopted* you and that makes you his son in a lot more than just a name on an official paper! How *dare* he do such a thing! Telling you you owe *him*, and making you feel guilty.'

'I don't feel guilty, Kitty – I'm happy to pay him back for as long as he says it'll take. Then I'll be rid of this thing and I'll be free to go my own way, make my own life.'

Her fingers tightened on his hand and her eyes glistened. 'And he thought you weren't

117

a good enough man to be allowed to take a courting interest in me!'

'He's a father, Kitty – wants the best for his daughter. You can savvy that.'

"Yes, I suppose so, but – well, it's Dad's outlook, and Lucas's, too, I guess. Just because you have Indian blood in you through no fault of your own... Oh, it becomes too tangled to keep on, Blaine! I admire you for what you're doing, even though I think you're foolish at the same time.'

'I'm glad I found you again, Kit – you seem really happy here.'

'I am–' She frowned slightly, looking a bit uncomfortable. 'Blaine – I – I'm staying here. This is worthwhile work, something I want to do. It would please me if you'd visit whenever you can, but I just want to make it clear that – we–'

He pressed her hand and stood up, almost smiling. 'It's enough that I know you're safe and happy and that I can see you from time to time– Morg's right, you know. I'm not good enough for you. I have nothing to offer you right now. But I'll make something of myself eventually. 1 know ranching pretty well and by the time I'm clear of Morg I don't doubt I'll know it a whole heap better. Then I'll start one of my own– I aim to gather some mavericks when I have the time and I know where I can keep 'em so I'll have the start of a herd of my own... Nothing says I can't do that or sell the cows myself and put away the cash... Just so long as I keep working at squaring-up with Morg.'

'That's a tremendous job to take on, Blaine!'

'I can do it.' He looked steadily at her with his one eye. 'Specially if I have some – incentive.'

She flushed and lowered her gaze. 'Blaine, I already told you...'

'I know. You're content here. Well, maybe you won't be forever – and I'll be waiting...'

She shook her head briefly. 'Blaine, I can't – promise anything like that! I – just – can't.'

'I know – but just remember anyway – I'll be around whenever you need me. Anytime.'

Her eyes were wet now and she even made a half-gesture as if she would throw her arms around him but didn't. He saw the pulse throbbing in her neck and knew her heart was hammering.

That was good enough for him: his words had moved her and because of her present position she was fighting not to let her emotions get the upper hand.

For now, it was just *'Howdy and Adios!'*

But there would come a time – he knew it. Sooner or later, they would be together.

Alamo Ames was talking with some of Don Miguel's *vaqueros* when Blaine rode back from the Mission *Seguridad*, trailed a brown-cloaked Father forking a weary looking burro. Alamo broke off his conversation and hurried out to meet Blaine, nodded and by-passed him, calling to the priest.

'Best hurry, *padre* – I think he's on his last.' Two of the *vaqueros* hurried to the priest and almost pulled him bodily from the burro. Then they practically carried him into the big glaring-white *hacienda*. Blaine swung down easily.

'The Don's going fast?'

Alamo nodded. 'The priest'll be lucky if he gets to the bedside in time.' Ames shifted his eyes over Blaine's usual unreadable face. 'Deliver them Jerseys OK?'

'Sure– A Sister Angelica took 'em off my hands.'

Ames shifted weight from one foot to the other. 'And...?'

'I had a mighty refreshing drink of lemon and lime – served to me by Sister Maria de Gracia.'

'Ah! So you met the young sister, uh?'

'Yeah – she's not a nun, not even a novice. Just a volunteer helper – seems quite content.'

Ames studied him carefully. 'Think she'll stay there?'

'I do.'

'Kind of a pity – a good-lookin' gal like that, hidin' her beauty under that drab old habit. Almost like she's – goin' to waste.'

'Don't see it that way. She's doing what she wants and is mighty happy about it. Good way to be.'

'Uh-huh... Well, guess there's nothin' to keep us here any longer. We'll head 'em out in the mornin'. OK with you?'

Blaine nodded and as Alamo started to turn away, he said, 'Thanks, *amigo*.'

Alamo just grunted and called to the remaining *vaqueros*. 'Hey, *amigos*– Let's get the *ganados* ready for the trail, eh? When we reach the Rio, the drinks are on me, OK?'

Judging by the grins and shouted remarks in Spanish that brought much laughter, it was definitely 'OK' with the Mexicans.

They pulled out as the first rays of the sun crept above the *cordillera* and stretched long shadows across the coolness of the land. The riders savoured this cool for they knew once the sun lifted properly into the sky, the sweat would pour from their bodies like water squeezed from a sponge.

A thousand head of sleek longhorns that had been nurtured with the patience and consideration only a solicitous – and indulgent – Spanish cattle-breeder could afford. Don Miguel had practically given them away – he sure had made a fine attempt at foiling his grasping kinfolk and Alamo was glad they would be a long way from here and safely back in the States when the fur started to fly once the old *hidalgo*'s will was read and the assets were totalled up.

They had eight men from the *rancho* and they knew their job. Blaine felt kind of superfluous on the drive but Alamo only grinned.

'The longhorns only speak Spanish down this way – these boys know 'em by name, practically, so we'll let 'em run things and just tag along for the ride.'

Blaine nodded but he was a man who liked to earn his keep, no matter who was providing it.

'You must have your knife pretty deep into old Morg by now, eh?'

Blaine frowned. 'You mean I hate him hard?'

'Hell, no one blames you – I mean, losin'

an eye's not exactly like gettin' a busted nose or a few loose teeth. He knew what Hardesty and Rendell were like when he turned 'em loose on you.'

'Well, he was mighty riled, 'cause he thought I was the one spoiled Kitty.'

Alamo frowned. 'You sound like you – *almost* like you – figure it was OK what he did.'

'Hell, no, but I can *savvy* why he did it.'

'OK, but you must still hate his guts.'

'He did a lot for me, Alamo – I'd've grown up with the Comanche if he hadn't taken me in.'

Alamo kept silent for a little while then sighed, nodding. 'Yeah – well, I guess that's you, Blaine. You aim to be free of him, but only after you figure you've squared away what he's done for you over the years. There has to be some cold hatred in there somewhere.'

'I'll do things my way,' Blaine said shortly and Alamo shrugged.

'Like always. But you sure got some queer notions of obligations. Anyone else would figure losin' an eye wiped out any debt to a man like Morg O'Day.' No reply from Blaine and Alamo murmured, 'But, I oughta know by now that you ain't any ordinary man...'

And that was proved soon enough.

Just two days later when they reached the Rio.

The herd was halfway across the ford just south of El Salto Vado, splashing through the shallow, yellowish water without fuss, for they had travelled contentedly with good graze along the trail from San Nicolas, when a bunch of screaming, painted Indians came sweeping out of the timber on the American side, shooting wildly.

From behind, on the Mexican side, another group of Indians rode out of the heat-cracked boulders like the flickering black tongue of a striking snake.

The herd – and the riders – were caught between two fast-closing jaws of a murderous pincer.

Blaine was already across on American soil and he slid his rifle out of its scabbard and turned to shout to the nearest *vaqueros*. There were four of them and they were already scattering, riding around the herd on the edge closest to the marauders.

Blaine breathed a sigh of relief: these men, for all their fancy rigs and clothes, their lazy style of riding herd, were fighting men and prepared to protect the cattle. That made things a hell of a lot easier he figured, throwing his Winchester to his left shoulder and sighting swiftly.

Lead whined overhead and he heard the thunk of a bullet taking a steer in the side, even saw the puff of dust as the animal lurched and began to bellow. Arrows zipped through the air and one that stuck in his saddle just beneath the horn he saw had a knapped flint tip. *Wild men, then – likely up from the Madres to the south, half-starved, just waiting for a herd to use the ford...*

It wasn't until a long time later that he realized this ford hadn't been used as a cattle crossing for a couple of years. Mostly it was freighters with their wagons and pack-mule trains who used the ford now. Most cattle were driven to the Gulf ports like Vera Cruz and then shipped to market on waiting sailing vessels.

But the Indians swept in determinedly and his rifle hammered methodically as he worked lever and trigger moving the smoking barrel a little each time, selecting his target.

Four horses went down with their riders who floundered in the river. Blaine cut across instantly and saw two *vaqueros* had the same notion. Between them, they drove a bunch close to forty steers into the shallows where the Indians were desperately trying to wade ashore. They all went down screaming under the hoofs or on the ends of the raking horns.

Blaine didn't wait to see the results. He swerved the sorrel, triggering his remaining shots in the rifle, sheathed the weapon and palmed up his six gun just as a painted, screaming face appeared right in front of him. The tomahawk whistled past his ear and he felt the jar as the hard knuckles of the brown hand wrapped around the handle hit the side of his neck. The Colt bucked in his hand, the barrel buried an inch deep into the leathery hide of the Indian. The blast blew the man clear off his horse and Blaine kicked it away, wheeled aside from a thrust with a lance and shot the man who wielded it somewhere in the face. The Indian swayed violently but managed somehow to stay in the saddle, riding away from the fight.

The river was churning, mud and froth tinged with red. The cattle's mournful bellows almost drowned out the war whoops and the crash of gunfire. It certainly overwhelmed Alamo's cursing as his horse blundered between two steers and, even as the trail boss yanked the horse's head up hard with his reins, he felt the horn slip into the heaving chest of his mount.

The horse started to go down and Alamo frantically kicked his boots free of the stirrups, actually jumped nimbly up on to the saddle and launched himself over the backs of the cattle. There were three lines of steers and he almost made it. His boot touched one and he used its instinctive humping to propel him on to the next to last line.

But the animals were wet with sweat and river water and a little blood on this particular steer. His boot slipped and if he yelled it wasn't heard above the bellowing and shooting.

Alamo slid out of sight between the lurching, shoving, crushing steers, slipped right down to where a tangled sea of legs thrashed and ripped up the river bottom.

The water in that area suddenly turned deep red.

Blaine had his rifle out again now, lean body twisting this way and that in the saddle: the Indians were trying to come up to him on his blind side. He had a two-handed grip on the hot barrel and he smashed it into the faces of two attackers, missed a third and, hanging on to his mount's neck, rowelled wildly, leaving it to the sorrel to crash a way through.

The horse made it, neck bleeding, a slash

of hide showing in a red lightning bolt on its right rump. Blaine straightened, holding the rifle in one hand, loosing off his last two shots in his Colt as a man charged in.

He didn't see if he hit target or not, kneeing the panting horse around instantly, yelling hoarsely to a pair of *vaqueros*, as he signalled frantically what he wanted them to do. They caught on immediately, joined him in a shallow arc and rammed their mounts into the flowing side of the brawling herd, shooting and yelling and kicking.

The steers, wild-eyed, frantic, attacked from all sides, veered away from their latest tormentors and started along the edge of the river on the American side. Blaine and his riders paced them, driving them on in stampede – straight at a bunched line of waiting Indians. These warriors had had the job of standing by, waiting for their fellow braves to drive the cowboys towards them where they could be cut down in a hail of withering fire.

Instead, all they saw was a wall of giant, snorting cows coming like demons from hell, horns glinting in the sun, some tipped with blood. They turned to run and Blaine and his *vaqueros* fired again and again. The herd smashed into the trailing riders, pulping them into the gravelly ground. Others screamed in terror and plunged back into the deeper part of the river, swimming their mounts desperately for the Mexican bank.

It was all over in another three minutes, the survivors of the raiders now all on the Mexican side, still riding, wanting to put as much distance between themselves and the devil herd as possible.

The men were wet and muddy and bloody and generally dishevelled but all stopped to fully reload their guns before a head-count was taken.

'*Dos hombres muerta,*' one man reported to Blaine who was looking around for Alamo, but couldn't see him anywhere – *two men dead*, the Mexican was telling him.

Another quick search found four other *vaqueros* were wounded and then a man farther along the bank called, '*Señor! Tres hombres – muerta!*' Three dead now...

The man pointed and Blaine rode back swiftly.

Even before he reached the huddle of bloody, torn rags half trampled into the mud, he knew he had found Alamo Ames.

# CHAPTER 9

## WELCOME BACK

Morgan O'Day looked down at the pile of gear on the end of his porch. A battered saddle with rifle sheath attached and the scratched, dented Henry rammed into it; a pair of spurs with the chrome plating coming off and one rowel badly bent; a few faded and patched work clothes in a weather-stained warbag, a threadbare blanket roll, a dented canteen and a pair of scuffed riding boots, worn over badly on the left heel. A jack knife with a broken blade point and a few coins sat in the middle of a crumpled kerchief.

O'Day lifted his gaze to Blaine leaning against a porch upright lighting a freshly-made cigarette. 'That's all Alamo left?' Blaine nodded and O'Day shook his head. 'After all those years – where you bury him?'

'Cemetery at Del Rio – I told the sawbones there to send the bill for patching-up the *vaqueros* to you.'

Morgan's eyes pinched down, but it was

Lucas who said, tone clipped, 'Big of you! They're Santiago's men.'

'He loaned 'em to us – besides he's likely dead by now.'

'Then his Estate can pay the bill – Goddamnit, Blaine, we're not responsible for every damn Mex who takes a bullet in an Indian raid!'

'I'll pay their bills,' Morgan said, sounding reluctant but uncomfortable under Blaine's hard stare.

'Aw, Pa, we don't have to! We're under no obligation to...'

'It's settled. Move on, Lucas – how many head did we lose, Blaine?'

'Twenty-seven, counting the six we had to shoot because of broken legs or horn gashes.'

'Goddlemighty!' breathed Lucas in disgust. 'We find a great chance to boost our herds cheaply and now you go and lose us nearly thirty head on a short trail drive like that!'

'Out of half a thousand,' Blaine said curtly.

'Just the same.' Lucas took on a sly look as he glanced at his father. 'Pa – that crossing at El Salto hasn't been used for cattle for a few years now. It's cheaper for the Mexes to drive to the Gulf and ship out by sea– Freighters use the crossing but I can't recollect the last time they got hit, because the Army usually gives 'em escort.'

They waited for Lucas to continue and there were beads of sweat on his face now. His eyes seemed to flick to Blaine and away again quickly, almost of their own accord.

'Well, seems to me that the first time in years a herd of really prime beef uses that crossin' it gets hit by Injuns – and we have here a man who's half-Comanche and has one helluva grudge against the O'Days...'

He didn't say more, knew there was no need. Blaine hadn't missed a drag on his cigarette or moved an inch. His stare nailed Lucas where he stood and made the man clearly uneasy, but he wouldn't look away even though the strain made his eyes water.

'Blaine?' asked Morgan tightly.

'They were renegade Apaches. From the Madres, I'd guess, where they been hiding out – reckon they were hungry enough to try for prime beeves, so it wouldn't cost anyone much to have 'em hit a herd using the crossing.'

'How much did it cost you?' sneered Lucas.

'Not a dime – I didn't hire 'em. But someone did.'

'Naturally!'

But Morgan frowned. 'You sound sure of that, Blaine.'

Blaine felt in his vest pocket, flipped a glinting coin towards Morg. The old man fumbled and dropped it but Lucas slowly picked it up, examining it as he handed it back to his father.

'Double eagle, Pa – current date, too, so it ain't some old one the Injun was carrying.' Lucas glanced at Blaine. 'You did find it on one of the dead Apaches, I guess...?'

Blaine nodded. 'Four more, too, but I gave a couple to the *vaqueros*, used the rest to bury Alamo.'

'So someone paid for that raid,' Morgan said, turning the gold coin between his fingers. 'A hundred dollars. A fortune to renegade bucks.'

'If they could find somewhere to spend it – not too many trading posts or stores in the Sierra Madres.'

'Only got your guess that that's where they were from. Could've made themselves look that way.' Lucas shrugged. 'Well, Pa, if he denies he paid it, your guess is as good as mine. Who did sick 'em onto our herd?'

Blaine moved so fast and silently that neither man was quite sure what had happened – least of all Lucas who found himself sitting in the dust at the foot of the porch steps, nursing a throbbing jaw, blinking in an attempt to settle his vision.

'What the hell'd you do that for?' demanded Morgan of Blaine, anger flaring in him like a brushfire, the old, knuckly fists clenching down at his sides.

'Ask Lucas.' Blaine stooped and picked up the jack knife with the broken blade. On the small metal oval let into the staghorn sideplates, the name 'Alamo' had been scratched. Blaine hefted it and put it in his pocket, plainly something to remember the dead trail boss by. He started down the steps and saw now that Lucas had a crooked smile on his lopsided face.

He knew then that Lucas was glad he had taken that punch in front of Morgan: it could only put Blaine further in the Old Man's black books.

'He figures I hired the Injuns to hit our herd, Pa. Just to make him look bad, inept,' Lucas said, as he swayed on his feet, watching Blaine walking away from the house. 'See how much he hates us O'Days...?'

Morgan grunted, watching Blaine, lips compressed. *You could never tell with that damn breed! His face was as blank as a granite cliff ... and he sure did hate the O'Days.*

'Best let me make the drive to San Antone, eh, Pa?'

Morgan rounded on his son as he came up on to the porch, dabbing at a bleeding lower lip now.

'No – Blaine can do it. Keep him out of my sight for a while.'

'Aw, now listen, Pa! I still reckon he had somethin' to do with the raid on that herd! You send him out on, the trail and – and – well, hell, who knows what he might arrange! I mean, the White Creek Reservation is in that general direction and that's where his tribe is.'

'And you reckon you could handle a raid by Blaine's Comanche friends? Even if he doesn't go on the drive, he could still arrange a raid ... right?'

Lucas agreed it was probably right. 'So why take the risk?'

'The herd's at risk whether he bosses it or not if what you're thinkin' is right – you got a man among the crew you can trust, really trust, I mean?'

'Well – Waco's done a few jobs for me before...'

'Didn't you send him down to Del Rio for somethin' recently?' Morgan asked, suddenly thoughtful.

Lucas tried to keep his face blank. 'Yeah – to pick up a pair of ridin' boots I'd ordered from that Mex leatherworker down there – but, sure, Pa, I could send Waco along on the drive to keep an eye on things. Likely cost a few bucks...'

'Pay him whatever he wants– It'll come out of your share of the herd money.' As Morgan swung back into the house, he flung over his shoulder to the stunned Lucas, 'You're the one with all the suspicions, right...?'

'Yeah – *right!*' gritted Lucas.

But he didn't say it out loud.

Inside, Morgan poured himself a stiff whiskey, glancing at the old cottage wall clock and wincing: he was starting earlier and earlier. But, dammit, he seemed to have more worries recently, day by day, than he'd had the past ten years.

And not the least of them was wondering if Blaine had found where Kitty was staying at that orphanage or whatever it was down there in Monterrey.

He didn't *think* Alamo would have broken his word not to tell where she was, but – well, Alamo was dead now and there was just no way of knowing.

He sure couldn't tell from anything Blaine said – or didn't say.

He tossed down the whiskey and immediately reached for the bottle again.

*Oh, Katy! Why did you have to saddle me with such a man as Blaine! He's gonna be the ruination of me, I can feel it ... I think I've known it for years!*

*And there ain't a damn thing I can do about it because I gave you my word I'd watch out for him... Now I gotta sit an' watch him work off his hatred for me...*

There were almost four thousand head in the herd when they started out for San Antone, a distance of about two hundred miles – as the crow flies. By the time they followed a trail that would provide water and feed for the cattle, it would be more than two hundred fifty miles, or even closer to three hundred, depending on conditions found along the way.

There hadn't been much rain of late and Calico Benedict, the rider Blaine had sent to scout on ahead, came back with the not-so-good news that the planned route would take them through country in the grip of drought.

'Some waterholes, Blaine,' Calico allowed, a man about the breed's age, but who had grown up in this country in a sod hut dug into a cutbank and could read the weather and topography like a book – except he couldn't read anything written but his own name, when he laboriously printed it on any papers he couldn't avoid signing.

'Grass?'

'Brown, mostly – short-stalk, too.'

Lucky Kinnane, in on the conversation, said, 'We got a couple spare buckboards, Blaine–We could load one with hay and feed and a couple salt-licks to help us out.'

'OK, Lucky. Good idea – set some men gathering hay, but not ones going on the drive.'

Lucky grinned. 'The boys'll love that, playin' sodbuster.'

Blaine headed for the barn to check out the condition of the buckboards, mentally choosing the horses he would use to pull the vehicle he picked as being the best of the two. The trail drive was going to cost more than Lucas had estimated so he went to see the man and told him Calico's news and Lucky's plan with the hay.

'Hell, Benedict's a worry-wort! Waco was out along that trail not long ago when he rode a chore for me. He never said nothing about dried-up creeks or short grass.'

'Calico knows the country between here and San Antone. Better than Waco – or you and me.'

'I'd take Waco's word...'

'Then take it. But there's been no rain so I'm taking the spare feed.'

Lucas glared as Blaine went about whatever business he had in mind, then hurried to see Morgan, painting a different picture for his father.

'He *wants* to take that hay along, Pa! You just think what a wagon-load of hay, suddenly bursting into flame at night, would do to a nervous trail herd—'

Morgan, hung-over from his drinking, was worried, and barely able to think. But he shook his head and said in phlegmy tones, 'No, Blaine's not like that – he – he's workin' off what he figures he owes me. Stoppin' me gettin' top price for the herd can't be in his plans. It'd work against what he's tryin' to do.' He added uncertainly, 'Whatever that is...'

'Well – I still think he'd take any chance that'd pull us down, Pa – he's an *Injun*, for Chrissakes! They never forgive a hurt, and Blaine was hurt plenty...'

Morgan was too irritable to be bothered with details and theories. He waved an angry arm at his son. 'Just let him ready the herd the way he wants! And quit botherin' me with all these damn notions you have! I know you've always hated his guts, been jealous of him, thinkin' I favoured him over you.'

'Well, that's sure true!'

'Ah! You're weak, Lucas. Weak and penny-pinchin' and jealous – and just plain miserable! I think you're even glad I disowned your sister! Now, get the hell outta here – I don't want to talk to you right now!'

Lucas went but he was fuming: to his warped way of thinking, Blaine had won yet another round!

But the son of a bitch would pay for it this time! By hell he would!

The large herd spread out once they cleared the big canyons.

The riders were mostly from Broken Wheel but some also from Bexley's Double B and Hurd's Twisted Horseshoe, small ranches which had cattle in with Morgan's drive.

The trail men were kept busy holding them in some semblance of order but it was pretty easy work at this stage. The cows had full bellies and had slaked their thirsts before setting out. Some would rather have slept it off under a shady tree but in general they moved willingly enough. Blaine headed them round to the south, skirting Brackettville and heading across towards Uvalde and the mining country.

Waco, Lucas O'Day's man, was a good enough cowboy, a tall, solid ranny in his mid-thirties with a rugged face and a pair of tiny eyes that made most folk think of a pig. But it was the look in those same eyes that prevented anyone but a damn fool from saying so out loud. Word had it that a couple of wranglers Waco had been drinking with in a bar in Bisbee, Arizona, started to feel their liquor and began making hog-snorting noises. The story claimed both were buried just outside the town and each crude sapling cross on the graves had a pig's head impaled upon it.

Someone, a little later, noted there were two notches cut into the butt of Waco's Colt .45.

Those notches stopped a lot of men wrangling with Waco. Blaine had no argument with the man, though – he did his chores well enough and kept mostly to himself. Fernando, who had come along to drive the wagon-load of hay, claimed it was because no one wanted to inadvertently tread on Waco's toes. Giving him a wide berth seemed the best way of avoiding this.

Now Blaine hauled his sorrel alongside

Waco's shaggy roan and told him to ride on ahead with Lucky and pick a good place for a night stop. The man simply nodded, spurred away to where Kinnane sat his mount under a tree, waiting, and then both rode on ahead and disappeared over a low ridge.

Campbell from Twisted Horseshoe, supposedly a part-owner with Martin Hurd of the small but growing spread, reined up alongside Blaine.

'Country's dry but not as bad as I thought – keep this up and it'll be a breeze gettin' to San Antone.'

'Lot of miles to travel yet, Cam.'

'Long as we get our bunch of five hundred in safely, I'll be happy.'

Campbell rode off and Blaine watched him go: *another one thinking only of himself ... wait till it came time to share costs of the hay and extra feed ... well, he'd worry about that when it happened...*

It was a good night camp and the grass was sweet, though the big herd had reduced it to stubble by sunup and, a couple hours later, three irate ranchers came spurring in, complaining.

'You goddamn trail drivers!' snarled a man about fifty with faded red hair hanging to his shoulders. 'We ain't seen any of you for years! Don't figure you're gonna start up again, stealin' our grass!'

'Open range, mister – check your survey maps and you'll find this is all Public Road through here.'

'That so?' The redhead squinted at Blaine. 'Breed, ain't you? Well, let me talk to the trail boss–'

'You're talking to him.'

'Judas! What kinda white man puts a breed in charge of his cows?' The redhead's companions growled their outrage, too. 'A one-eyed one at that!'

The man's friends laughed but Blaine simply sat more easily in the saddle and slapped his right hand against his thigh, close to his holstered six gun. 'I'll tell you his name – it's Morgan O'Day of Broken Wheel – and I'm his adopted son, Blaine–'

He watched, deadpan, as the colour drained from all three faces. The redhead swallowed, looked at his companions who seemed ready to turn their horses and ride off.

'But I'm the one here,' Blaine added quietly, 'so I'm the one you deal with – now, where were we...?'

The redhead spat. 'Forget it – I've heard

about you. Morg O'Day, too. But he don't usually drive his cows across our range.'

'*Public* range, remember, Red? I just told you: go check your survey maps and see – now go do that and we'll forget the whole thing...'

Red was happy enough with that and so were his pards, but he was reluctant to show it – until Blaine sighed and lifted his hand to his gun butt. Then he wheeled his mount and galloped off after the others.

Waco, coming up slowly, staring at Blaine, said quietly, 'Facin' down three hardcases like them ranchers took some doin'...'

'I noticed you were just waiting to jump in and lend a hand,' Blaine said and Waco flushed for he had had no such intention. 'Go help Fernie haul in some wood for a big fire – think I heard wolves in those trees yonder.'

'Gatherin' firewood ain't my job!'

'It is when I tell you it is – you want to go back to Broken Wheel? I can tell you to do that, too.'

Waco didn't want to leave this herd yet – he'd been paid half his money already by Lucas and he aimed to collect the other half as well. He jerked his horse's head around savagely and spurred after Fernando who was swinging along, whistling, an axe over

144

his shoulder, making for the line of timber.

Up around Uvalde, the grass thinned drastically and the naked red convolutions of the hills were hard on the eyes. The herd travelled down on the flats but even here they could smell the dust raised by the hopeful miners honeycombing the hillsides with shafts and tunnels.

It was hot and dusty, men, horses and cows were all parched. Then Calico rode back to say the waterholes he had checked out previously had shrunk considerably, but there was likely enough to water the herd if they did it in small, tight groups, keeping the main herd out of sight of the water over a rise.

This worked well enough although the water was of low quality. But it kept the herd slogging along and a couple of days later, staying south of Hondo, they came to the usually deep-flowing White Creek. But the water was way down and some cattle bogged on the crossing, though they only lost three.

'Gonna be drier up around San Antone,' said Blaine to Kinnane a day later. He knew this part of the country: the Comanche Reservation was not far away, back in the hills. 'And they're mighty thirsty – if they get a sniff of water anywhere they'll be damn impossible to stop.'

Calico had brought the news that the waterholes he had scouted were now no more than bogs.

'Not gonna be able to risk givin' 'em a drink here, Blaine,' Kinnane said.

'No, some are bound to smell the wet mud and they charge in there, they'll be up to their bellies in nothin' flat and we'll end up shootin' 'em.'

Blaine had seen this kind of thing happen before. There was only one thing to do – but his decision to keep driving the herd on through the night so as to be well clear of the muddy waterholes come morning was not a popular one.

Keeping so many cows on the move in pitch darkness was no easy matter and it meant every man, including the cook and Fernando, had to take his turn at riding herd.

'Oughta get extra pay for this!' Waco growled and some of the others who, most likely hadn't thought about that aspect until it was mentioned, grumbled their agreement. 'By hell, we oughta!'

Waco hoped this further attempt of his to stir up trouble and unrest would get back to Lucas – he might be able to squeeze a few extra dollars out of him, too, if he pulled off his other part of the chore successfully. He

146

looked around at the bunched men drinking coffee and eating cold-cuts and jerked beef: tonight Blaine didn't want a fire at all. The cows were too spooked from the long, dry trail and now to be pushed on when they figured to rest... Anything could happen when they were in this kind of mood.

And it did.

About two in the morning they rested a spell, the scent of green leaves coming from somewhere up ahead which might mean water. The cattle, perversely, didn't want to stop now after smelling the trees and the riders were having a tough job trying to keep them bunched.

'Don't let 'em break!' Blaine called, working the sorrel after two steers that were trying to make a run for it. He slapped one across the eyes with his coiled lariat and kicked the other hard behind the ear, turning both back into the edges of the main herd. Panting, sweating, he called, 'Ah, we're gonna wear ourselves out trying to hold 'em, dammit!'

There was a lot of riding and shouting and no one could say where another was exactly – just shadows, moving swiftly against the stars. The night was humid which might mean that a storm was brewing. Blaine thought he had glimpsed a flare of light running along the horizon earlier, but it had been on his right side and by the time he had fully turned to check, it had gone.

So no one saw Waco fire the hay wagon with a weary, sleeping Fernando in the driver's seat, allowing the tired team to make its own pace and direction as he nodded and swayed with the jerky rhythm of the over-loaded vehicle.

The first Fernando knew of it was when the flames leapt ten feet high and Waco, just a dark figure, hauled him roughly out of the driving seat, still mostly asleep, and smashed him brutally into the ground. The team hit the traces with a jarring slam as Waco threw some burning hay onto their backs and then it was too late.

Someone yelled so frantically his voice cracked high and panicky like a child's, 'Stam – peeeeede!'

The fiery wagon was bouncing in amongst the cattle now and they exploded all over the plains, horns raking at riders' mounts and each other, bellowing and bawling in fear, eyes rolling whitely, hoofs raising a thunder that shook the earth, loose red dust blinding the riders as they tried to regain control.

But the herd was loose now and ripping

the night apart like a burlap curtain, inter-mittently lit by the wagonload of fire which, eventually, crashed onto its side and spread a river of flames into the rear of the herd.

Nothing could stop them now.

And over the general commotion, Blaine heard someone yell wildly, panicky,

'Hell almighty! Injuns! Dozens of 'em. Injuns! Injuns...!'

# CHAPTER 10

## FRAME-UP

There were Indians, all right, just visible as some raced to get behind the herd and were lit by the dying flames of the hay wagon.

No one noticed if they wore any paint or not, but they were letting loose with their war-whoops and riding as if they were part of the night wind. Some held rifles, others lances, and others bows and arrows.

A gun or two hammered as they swept in on the herd and bows twanged as arrows drove into plunging, snorting steers that barely resembled the compliant animals that had been driven up from Broken Wheel only days earlier. With rolled-back whites of eyes and horn tips catching fugitive flashes of light, wet mucus flying from distended nostrils and heads tossing, big bodies gyrating acrobatically, they resembled some of the beasts in the wildest imaginings of artists who liked to portray Hell as men could expect to find it.

Blaine was yelling, almost bursting a blood vessel in his neck, as he rode in when his men began shooting at the Indians. He was in danger of being shot for he was now between the cowboys and the redskins. His men cursed, threw their aim, wrenched running mounts aside. Whatever he was yelling was drowned in the general din.

Then an Indian was shot and somersaulted off his horse. Another lurched, dropping his lance, arm dangling. Suddenly, arrows were zipping across the heaving backs of the herd and a cowboy grunted, grabbing at a shaft quivering in his thigh. Another swore when his hat was impaled and torn from his head. A third's mount reared, arrow in the chest.

'The herd! The herd!' Someone at last was able to distinguish Blaine's words. 'Save the herd!'

'Is he loco?' bawled Waco, glaring at Calico Benedict thundering alongside. 'We save the cows and the goddam Injuns'll nail us!'

'I dunno, Waco,' Calico called back, starting to haul on his reins. 'Somethin' queer about them Injuns – they weren't shootin' at us till we nailed a couple of them!'

'Are you loco, too?'

Waco swung away, Winchester coming up to his shoulder as he started blazing at the redskins who seemed no more than fleeting shadows now, riding here and there, lying along their mustangs' backs – and shooting into the herd! But not killing the animals, shooting so as to drive them together, forcing them to bunch and actually slow down...

Waco, frowned, holding his fire, but wheeling wildly as he saw one Indian raising his old trade rifle. The Texan triggered and the Indian was blasted off his mount and fell into the edge of the herd.

Blaine was riding everywhere, yelling at his men who blinked at him uncertainly and then it became apparent that the cows were being wheeled in a wide arc that was gradually tightening in the legendary 'wheel of steers', a method used by the old-timers in desperation to stop a stampede. It was said to have been first successfully attempted by a man named Shakes Mulvane, a Black Irishman who, inflamed by some of his own *poteen* – some claimed his horse was drunk, too – turned his herd on the very edge of a cliff by forcing them into a circle, intermingling leaders with stragglers in a gradual milling until they came to rest. He lost no more than two dozen over the edge – out of almost three thousand head.

Someone said later that he had gotten the idea from the old Plains Indians who sometimes used the manoeuvre when hunting buffalo... Now, *these* Indians were forming the mill wheel and the stunned and puzzled cowboys reined down slowly as the red men rode in among the bawling cattle, gentling them with nudges from moccasined feet or the horn-tipped end of a bow, the butt of a lance.

'Now I really got somethin' to tell my grandkids if I ever have any!' breathed Lucky Kinnane, looking around for Blaine.

But Blaine was already talking with two of the Indians, one big warrior, the other shorter with a horseface but looking very powerful. There were gestures and signs and finally grins and Blaine and the two Indians slapped each other on the back. He pointed to one corner of the herd and the Indians rode that way with their men following, some warily watching the white men who still held guns.

As the trail crew watched, slack-jawed in surprise, Blaine directed them to cutting out about thirty prime steers.

'Christ, he's gone plumb loco!' growled Waco. He looked around at the bunched white men. 'The son of a bitch is *givin'* 'em all them prime beeves! *Our* beeves!'

He started to move across, the others hesitatingly following. Blaine reined up, lifting a hand.

'Easy, boys – just rewarding the Comanche for their help.'

'Help!' exclaimed Waco. '*Help* he says! Christ, they were tryin' to shoot us and steal the goddam cattle! Where the hell's the help there? Except to themselves!'

Blaine shifted his one eye to Waco and the man let his words drift off. 'Lucky, take some men and collect the strays and ride herd so they don't cut loose again. We'll camp here tonight – not you, Waco. You stay here.'

Waco swung back. 'You know them Injuns, don't you? You was happy-talkin' with them two big sonuvers...'

'Running Bird and Longhead,' Blaine cut in. 'My blood brothers.'

'Hey, you rannies hear that?' Waco called. 'These Injuns are his *blood brothers!* This was a set-up!'

Lucky Kinnane and the others had stopped now. They were even more surprised when Blaine admitted Waco was right.

'Sure – sent word to Running Bird to have some men standing by when we entered White Creek country. I had a notion we were going to have trail trouble – and they were to be ready to ride in and help us out. Which they did, and for which I've rewarded 'em.'

'Morg's gonna love this!' crowed Waco.

'It'll come out of my share,' Blaine said easily. 'And, Waco, Fernie says you dragged him out of that burning wagon and slugged him unconscious.'

'Well – yeah! I seen it was on fire an' he was asleep in the goddamn drivin' seat, so I hauled him out before he got burned... I was gonna try an' drive it from the herd...' Blaine's gaze was steady and Waco made his face hard, curling his lips, as he glared back. 'You can't prove different!'

'Guess not – no more'n I can *prove* you fired the hay wagon, but I know damn well you did. Maybe even on Lucas' orders...'

'You're a goddamn liar!'

154

The words splashed into the dusty night air like a rock falling into a pool. There was a hushed silence that rippled through the riders and Waco was already aware that he had gone too far: call a man a liar out here and you better have your gun half-way out of leather. He didn't give Blaine a chance, rammed his horse into the breed's sorrel, and snatched at his six gun. Blaine was unseated and grabbed at Waco's gun arm, twisted as he continued to fall, dragging the cursing Texan with him.

They hit hard and Waco lost his grip on his Colt and swung his free hand in a backward blow. It knocked Blaine's hat off, coming in as it did on his right side, and then Waco's jaw seemed to explode off his face, leaving him half-blinded as his eyeballs rolled in their sockets and pain shot through his neck and upper spine. A second blow almost tore his head off his shoulders – he said later – and he went over backwards, but kicked out instinctively. Whether by accident or design it came in on Blaine's eyeless side and took him on the temple, knocking the eyepatch askew and the watching cowpokes glimpsed the mangled socket for the first time. Blaine sat down, started to rise a little groggily, and Waco launched himself bodily, clubbing with his right fist. Blaine took one blow and went down flat, brought up his knees into Waco's midriff as the man crowded him.

Blaine straightened his legs and Waco groaned as he rolled to one side, scrabbling in his winded efforts to get up. He made it halfway, and then Blaine lunged, right fist striking with the force of a sledgehammer smashing into rock. Waco completely somersaulted, face dragging in gravel as he skidded down the slight slope. He moaned and rolled his head a little, but didn't get up. Blaine kicked him hard and Lucky Kinnane steadied him as he stood, handed him a canteen. 'I seen Waco trailin' that hay wagon for quite a spell, twice had to tell him to get back on point.'

Blaine rinsed his mouth, then drank, panting. He nodded. 'He's Lucas' man.'

Kinnane stiffened. 'Surely you ain't sayin'...'

'Said all I'm gonna for now – let's get these cows settled for the night. We'll make the run into San Antone tomorrow.'

'What about him?' Kinnane gestured to the unconscious Waco.

'Leave him – he can follow or not. But far as I'm concerned, he's all through.'

Waco didn't join up with the rest of the Broken Wheel men although Lucky Kinnane and Calico saw him in one of the San Antone saloons, drunk and on the prod.

Because of his swollen, crooked jaw, he spoke with a slur and the barkeep changed shift with a new man just as Waco emptied his glass. He ordered another, and while the previous man had learned what Waco was drinking, this man asked three times what it was he wanted.

'You wanna talk with a foot in your mouth, mister, I ain't got time to listen. Other customers're waitin'...'

Waco's left hand darted out, grabbed the man's fresh, clean shirt and hauled him back. The 'keep swore when the shirt sleeve tore. He reached under the counter for his billy and Waco drew his Colt and laid it across the man's head – not once, but back and forth three or four times. The barkeep's face was a torn, bloody mess by the time he sagged to the floor.

Men waiting for bar service growled and turned threateningly towards Waco. He backed up, Colt still in his hand, thumb on the trigger now.

'U'll shoot yuh ull!' he slurred, easing towards the side door. He waved the Colt, hammer back now, and the men stopped.

'Go on!' one bearded man growled. 'Git – before we stomp you into the sawdust!'

Waco slid out of the side door, fired a couple of shots into the air, and the men scattered. He had gone by the time they wrenched open the door.

'Mean sonuver that Waco, when he's riled,' opined Calico.

'Yeah,' Lucky Kinnane said thoughtfully. 'Reckon Blaine's gonna have trouble with him yet...'

Kinnane was right – and the trouble was waiting for Blaine when he arrived back at Broken Wheel.

He'd left the crew in town to have a few drinks – on him as promised – before returning to the ranch, and as he dismounted stiffly in the early evening Clay Winton called from the bunkhouse,

'Where're the boys, Blaine?'

'Let 'em stay in town to wash the dust outta their throats – you fellers can go on in if you like – put it on my bill but be back here by midnight.'

The off-duty men needed no second invitation and even the cook banked his fires and rode with them as they whooped and hollered their way towards the town road.

As Blaine mounted the porch steps Lucas stepped out of the shadows. 'Someone make you ramrod?'

'No – but I reckon they'll've earned a drink or two, the way you work 'em. Keep 'em happy.'

Lucas grunted. 'Pa wants to see you right away.'

The Old Man was waiting in his office and Blaine was surprised to find Waco there, too. The man's face showed signs of his beating, but he managed a crooked grin that warned Blaine he was in for some trouble.

'How much'd you get for the herd?' demanded Morgan without preamble. Blaine heard the faint slurring of his words, surprised – Morg was already well on the way to getting drunk: a state he seemed to favour lately. Blaine took some crumpled papers from his vest pocket, smoothed them out and dropped them on to the desk in front of the rancher.

Morgan scanned the figures swiftly, adjusting his wire-framed eye-glasses. He looked up. 'Work out how much a head that comes to – then multiply it by thirty.' He took off the glasses and set his granite gaze on Blaine as Lucas entered the office.

'That's how much comes out of your share.'

Blaine nodded. 'Already calculated that – was worth it to save the herd.'

Morgan swivelled his gaze to Waco. 'That what he was doin'?'

'He says!' Waco said, scowling. 'He had to try and save face some way! – he had them Injuns waitin' to stampede the herd and rustle all they could before we could round-up the cows again – but the stampede got tangled up and stopped early... He had to do somethin', so he came up with this hog-wash about havin' the Injuns waitin' to help out – *in case there was trouble.*'

'And that's your story, uh?' Morgan grated, boring his gaze into Blaine again. *'In case there was trouble.'*

'Figured there could be – after Lucas' stampede went wrong at El Salto.'

'Damn you, Blaine! I had nothing to do with that!'

Morgan held up a hand for his son to calm down. 'You got a fair price in San Antone, but I don't care for this stuff with the Injuns.'

Blaine waited.

'Your tribe, weren't they?' Blaine nodded and Morgan sat back in his chair. 'Don't look good, does it?'

'Depends what you believe.'

'I believe it seems mighty strange that he left the crew in town, Pa – like keep 'em outta the way so they can't tell *their* side of the stampede story – and tomorrow, after he's paid for their booze...' He shrugged. 'They'll likely go along with anythin' he says.'

'That's a nice, devious mind you got there, Lucas,' opined Blaine.

'Why'd you beat-up on Waco?' asked Morgan, scowling.

'For setting fire to the hay wagon.'

'I never did that!' Waco snapped, rubbing his aching jaw, looking at Lucas first, then Morgan. 'Boss, I just happened to be the one saw it burnin' – and I saved that damn lazy Mex's hide! Ask me, he coulda started it, tossed a cigarillo butt into it or some-thin'.'

'Fernie doesn't smoke,' Blaine said quietly.

'I've seen him smoke!' Waco said force-fully, turning to Lucas who nodded slowly.

'Believe I have, too.'

Blaine's face gave nothing away.

'Or it coulda been a fire arrow from them damn Injuns you had waitin',' Waco allowed, looking pleased with himself at the notion. 'Hell, there was lightnin' about – fire arrow coulda dropped right into that hay

161

durin' a lightnin' flash – I reckon them Injuns'd be rat-cunnin' enough to time it just right.'

'You're pushing a wagon uphill with the brakes on, Waco,' Blaine said. 'Why don't you get outta here before I throw you out?'

Morgan's eyes blazed. 'The hell you think you are, mister! This is my office! I'll say who stays and who goes – and right now I reckon it'd be better for you to go. I'll see you in the mornin' and if you got nothin' particular to do before you turn in, you might pack your warbag... Just in case...'

Morgan's face was like the sky before a twister of devastating size swept in: cold, dark, implacable, and deadly dangerous. He was reckless now, as well as mad, prepared to cut his losses by firing Blaine if the moment suited him.

Blaine let his single eye rake across Waco and come to rest on Lucas, who flushed uncomfortably.

'See you in the morning then, Morg – matter of fact, I think I'll ride into town and have a few drinks with the boys.'

They watched him go and then Morgan, mouth dry, unable to hold off any longer, stood and went to his cupboard. He poured three stiff drinks, tossed his down and poured another. He jerked his head at Waco who took a glass for himself and handed the other to Lucas.

'You really thinking of kicking that breed off Broken Wheel at last, Pa?' Lucas sounded eager for an affirmative.

Morgan drank and sloshed more whiskey into his glass. Waco gestured to Lucas, arched his eyebrows and nodded towards Morgan – who saw him and snarled. 'What's that mean? That stupid look you've got on your face?'

Waco, taken by surprise, bristled. 'It ain't stupid – *I* ain't the one gettin' pie-eyed.'

Morgan ground his teeth. 'Out! Get him out of here, Lucas! Kick him off the place! I've had a bellyful of him!'

Waco glared at Lucas. 'Wait a minute! I'm owed money here! We had a deal, Luke!'

'Shut up!' gritted Lucas but he saw his father stiffen: there was nothing wrong with the Old Man's hearing,

'What's this? What "deal"?'

Lucas grinned crookedly. 'Not "deal" really, Pa...'

'Yeah! a goddamn *deal!*' Waco snapped. 'You promised me two hundred bucks, minimum, if I...'

'Shut up, damn you!' Lucas squared up to

his father, heart pounding. 'Look – I had a hunch Blaine was gonna try somethin' with that herd – I knew he was going through White Creek where his Injun friends are so I just told Waco to keep an eye on things ... and to report back to me.'

Morgan had even forgotten he was holding an empty glass in one hand and part-bottle of whiskey in the other as he narrowed his eyes. 'Two hundred bucks – just for that? You're lyin', boy! An' you know what I think of liars and what I do to 'em!'

That startled Lucas and his heart beat even faster. *Christ, the whippings he'd taken when he was growing up – the humiliation of having to drop his trousers and have his butt welted by the Old Man's belt in front of the men – in front of Blaine!*

*Never again!* He'd sworn it when he turned twenty that never again would the Old Man lay a hand on him that way. He glanced at Waco, saw the man's stupid look, wondering just what kind of a clash he was going to see between father and son here – something to talk about, to spread all over Texas in his drunken rantings...

'I ain't lying!' Lucas shouted at his father, his face reddening, shocking himself at his temerity. But it was too late now to with-

164

draw the words and his father's jaw jutted, he hurled his bottle and glass into a corner and turned and reached for a bridle where it hung on the wall.

'*No!*' shouted Lucas. 'You ain't gonna whup me, Pa!'

'Drop your trousers, boy!'

Morgan strode around the desk, bridle raised and Lucas made a whimpering sound, snatching at his gun. Morgan's eyes widened at first, then narrowed to mocking slits. 'You don't have that much guts, boy!' And he slashed with the bridle. Lucas jumped back and the leather tore the gun from his shaking hand. He threw up his arms, whimpering as the old terror of his youth came flooding back. Until the thunder of three deliberate shots filled the room.

Slowly, he lowered his arm from across his eyes and he saw his father on the floor, blood pooling around his head and crawling from two holes in his back. Lucas, white and trembling, turned and saw the smoking pistol in Waco's fist.

'Jesus! You've killed him!'

The man smiled crookedly. He stepped forward and dropped something on the floor by Morgan's body.

It was a jack-knife with a broken blade

point with 'Alamo' scratched into a metal oval on the staghorn handle.

'Blaine must've dropped it in his hurry to get away after killin' Old Morg... Right, Luke?'

It seemed a long time, but in the end Lucas nodded.

'Reckon it'll cost you more than two hundred, though,' Waco said confidently.

Lucas grinned crookedly. 'I reckon so – but it'll be worth every cent!'

## CHAPTER 11

## TRAIL'S END

Blaine regretted his snap decision to ride into Brackettville and join the crew of Broken Wheel.

He was tired from the long trail drive and the seemingly endless ride back from San Antone. Squeezing a halfway decent price for the herd out of the meathouse agents had taken a lot of effort – he wasn't a man who did much talking and it had been two long day's hard drinking and fast talking before the agent had come around.

Then he had done it so abruptly and with such good humour that Blaine knew the man had just been filling in time, enjoying the endless hassling and bargaining.

Well, truth was, he was tired of a lot of things lately. Tired of Broken Wheel and Morgan and Lucas – particularly Lucas. But he had given his word he would work off what Morgan figured he owed him and although he knew it had been a rash decision he would not go back on what he had undertaken.

He was not a man given to wild drunks – he didn't care for the rotgut whiskey they served that much, although he liked beer when it was iced – but the crew had a couple of hours start when he arrived and plied him with drinks. He shook his dark mood deliberately and tossed down more whiskey in half an hour than he had, probably, drunk over the last couple of months. He had a few beers as well, felt suddenly expansive, and bought cigars all round. The strong tobacco mixed with the vile liquor soon made his head swim.

The men were drunk, mostly happily so, but a couple got into fights with townsmen. Then someone started singing trail ditties and everyone joined in – making up their own words and causing much coarse laughter. The bar girls moved in through the smoky fog and soon were helping staggering men upstairs to their musty beds. Others were content to dance with the 'ladies' – at least until roving female hands aroused basic instincts and gave them other ideas.

Blaine refused to dance – his head was swimming and he felt queasy, unused to this kind of thing – but at least he had stopped worrying about the O'Days, although he felt kind of sad when he allowed himself to dwell on Kitty...

'Go on, Blaine! Dance!' urged Lucky Kinnane, swaying, with a straggly-haired blonde a good twelve years his senior clinging to his arm, trying to steer him towards the stairs.

'Yeah, *dance*, *Blaine!*' urged the brassy whore, false smile pasted on, shaking him a little. 'Let's see you dance.'

He shook free, a little unsteady. 'You wanna see a dance?' he roared and a wave of silence washed through the big bar, all eyes turning to the one-eye breed, surprised: everyone was used to his quiet, deep voice, not this stentorian bellow. 'I'll show you a dance you've never seen before!'

He overturned a couple of tables, kicked

chairs out of the way and began a grunting chant, stamping in time to it, lifting one leg, hopping a little on the other foot, lowering the leg and raising the other, all the time his arms jerking and his lean body twisting as he moved in a tight circle.

'By God!' screamed the whore, laughing. 'He's dancin', all right! He's doin' a god-damned *war dance! Watch out!*'

It suited the mood of the drunks and they began shouting and whooping, clapping their hands and stamping their feet. Calico and Lucky and Clay Winton joined Blaine and the four of them were busy raising the roof with their clamour when a gunshot brought things to an abrupt halt.

Blearily, they stared at the batwings. Sheriff Marsh Kilgour, stooped a little from his arthritis, hatless, and his thinning grey hair loose and wild, stood there, holding a smoking six gun. Blaine's blurred smile of amusement faded slowly as Lucas and Waco pushed in behind the lawman, both looking mighty pleased with themselves.

Kilgour limped down the silent room, one hip giving him a lot of trouble lately, and stood before Blaine.

'Well, guess we don't see you like this very often, Blaine. Fact, don't recollect *ever*

169

seein' you like it before.' He squinted. 'This a tribal celebration or somethin', mebbe?'

Blaine shrugged. 'Celebratin' – drownin' my sorrows – something like that, Marsh. Have I broken the Law?'

'No-ooo – not with your cuttin' loose the curly wolf, leastways, but back at Broken Wheel you sure busted it good.'

Blaine, sobering fast, frowned and flicked his single-eyed gaze to the smirking Lucas and Waco. *Those two were up to something –* that much seeped through his sodden brain but he wasn't prepared for Marsh Kilgour's next words.

'I'm arrestin' you for the murder of Morgan O'Day– Now you gonna gimme trouble or come along quietly...?'

The hard, narrow streaks of the iron bars on the window gradually took form as the sky lightened in the east. From down the stone corridor he heard the clatter of tin mugs and the rattle of dishes, and he smelled frying bacon. Then came the deputy's heavy boots trudging towards his cell.

Blaine sat up slowly, wincing, holding his head as he swung his feet to the floor.

'Ain't used to tyin' one on, eh?' Deputy Linus Sebastian grinned through the bars.

'Stay put while I open the door and slide your breakfast in... Nice greasy bacon and soft-fried eggs with burnt toast and coffee that'll float a six-shooter. Mebbe a couple flies – for fresh meat!'

'You can keep everything but the coffee,' slurred Blaine as the deputy opened the door partially and slid the tray along the flagged floor. Half the coffee spilled into the tin platter of bacon and eggs but it couldn't spoil it any more than it already was.

'You'll be required to come out for wash-up at six o'clock,' intoned Linus, locking up again. 'Then you can clean out the other cells and muck-out the stables... Sheriff don't ride much no more but he still keeps a couple fine hosses– Likes to talk to 'em and think about the old days when he was an Injun fighter. Whoops! Did I say "Injun" or "engine"?'

'Just go away, Deputy, and let me die in peace.'

The java was the worst Blaine had ever tasted and he couldn't even look at the mess on the tray let alone attempt to eat it. He rolled and lit a cigarette but stubbed it out almost immediately. Then he rattled the bars until Linus Sebastian came striding down angrily, demanding to know what all the racket was about.

'Lemme wash-up now and I'll get started on the chores,' Blaine said. 'I'll go loco if I have to stay in here smelling that pigswill.' He pointed to the bacon and eggs.

'Matter of fact the pigs kinda like my cookin', but Uncle Marsh says to have you wash-up at six in the a.m. and... Aw, what the hell? C'mon out an' get started...'

At the wash bench the chill water in the tin bowl woke Blaine up fully and he sluiced it over his face and head several times. Drying himself on the towel, he saw Linus watching from the doorway.

'Stables next... I got a long-handled shovel for you so you don't have to get your hands dirty. Not that it'd bother you much I s'pose. You'd be used to sleepin' in trash and manure at the Reservation, wouldn't you?'

Sebastian was new here, had come up from El Paso with Marsh Kilgour's widowed sister and landed the deputy's job. 'Yeah, Linus, we're like that – sleep where we can. Muck don't bother us Injuns.'

'Hell, I dunno how you can stand it,' Linus sneered. The new deputy was feeling superior now, white man over breed, and Blaine deliberately sniffed, spat on the floor before going through the door.

'Pig! They say you shot your own father.'

'I never shot anyone. But the one who got killed was the man who raised me, not my real father. *He* shot *him* in a raid on our camp when I was a shaver.'

'Ah! But finally got your revenge, eh? Well, they say you people've got a helluva lotta patience...' He gestured abruptly. 'That clapboard buildin' yonder. Put the hosses out to grass first.'

Blaine took the long-handled shovel and inspected the blade, metal worn shiny and thin from use. 'This is too rounded and worn to shovel manure and straw.'

Linus' face hardened – as much as it could, him being moon-faced and flabby. He dropped a hand to his six gun, trying hard to be the tough deputy. 'You just do what you're told!'

'Sure.' Then Blaine jabbed the end of the long handle hard into Linus's flabby belly and the man grunted, staggered, and before he could get his balance, Blaine hit him across the head with the flat of the blade. Linus dropped like a poled steer and Blaine dragged him quickly into the stable, bound his wrists and ankles with spare harness and stuffed the man's own neckerchief in his drooling mouth. He tied it into place with a sleeve ripped from the deputy's shirt.

Blaine took the man's gun with him, ran back into the jail building and found his own Colt and Winchester in the front office with his saddle. After locking the door, he took these back to the stables, chose the roan and saddled quickly. In minutes, he led the horse through the gap in the sagging paling fence, around a cess pool and into the brush. He cleared town before many folk were astir. He hoped Marsh Kilgour's arthritis was giving him hell this morning so he would sleep in and not come down to the jailhouse to check on Linus for a few hours yet.

It was noon before the posse arrived at Broken Wheel.

Sheriff Marsh Kilgour was leading, taking swigs of strong 'pain killer' from a silver flask he carried because his arthritis was troubling him. Linus Sebastian was there, too, his hat on all askew because one side of his head was swollen. He was bitching about the headache he had sustained and maintained that he ought to have stayed behind in town.

'You let him escape,' Kilgour told him unsympathetically. 'Only right you help recapture him.'

There were six townsmen, none very enthusiastic, but they had been forcibly deputized by the sour old sheriff.

Lucas was in his father's office – avoiding looking at the dark stains on the floor that had so far resisted all efforts to remove them. He was going over the books and felt his sombre mood rapidly dissipating as he saw the still-incomplete figures, but figures that promised him almost instant riches.

After all, he was the lone beneficiary of Morgan's will now. Kitty had been disowned months ago and Blaine would soon be hanged for Morg's murder–

Then he heard the posse and his belly lurched. He called for Waco who had been searching the house, on Lucas' orders, for money the Old Man might've had stashed away for an emergency – Lucas knew there *had* to be some...

*A lot with a little luck!*

Kilgour didn't dismount, called for Lucas to come out on to the porch. The sheriff was gripping the saddlehorn firmly and swayed slightly. Lucas compressed his lips. *Goddamnit! Marsh was already halfway drunk...* Which meant he would be unpredictable.

*Damnit! He didn't need this!*

Marsh didn't mince his words. 'Saddle up – this sorry son of a bitch of a nephew of mine let Blaine escape. He's ridin' my roan – can pick its tracks out of a bunch of a hundred mustangs easy. He's headed into the hills yonder.'

'I can't come now!' Lucas said, heart racing. 'I – I've a lot of paperwork to do and Morg's funeral to arrange and...'

'His murderer to catch – I'd have to think you don't care whether he's caught or not, Lucas, if you refuse to come.'

Lucas mentally cursed the drunken old fool. 'Waco – saddle some horses and grab a few men– We'd better scour the hills with the sheriff's posse before he gives us a bad name – that satisfy you, Marsh?'

'I can always call in a few more men if I need 'em from some of the out-lyin' spreads...'

It was hot, unproductive work. They found tracks where Blaine had skirted the Broken Wheel down by the riverbend. An ex-army scout named Tyson was tracking for Kilgour and he said he couldn't be certain, but looked to him like Blaine had crossed the river.

So they crossed over, then broke up into

two parties and arranged to meet near Fool's Canyon at sundown.

'Hell, you aim to stay out that long?' Lucas complained.

'Long as it takes – Lucas, this is your father's *killer*. Figured you'd ride to hell'n'back to track him down.'

'Well, sure I would – but I know Blaine. I figure he'll be riding hell-for-leather for White Creek. His Injun kin'll hide him, no trouble.'

'I've already wired the San Antone Marshal to get a posse out there and some men up to the Reservation.' The sheriff paused to take a final, deep swig of pain-killer from his flask, watery eyes on Lucas. 'My creaky ol' bones tell me he's still around here. He maintains you framed him for Morg's murder, Lucas, you and Waco–'

'Well, he would say something like that, wouldn't he?'

'Mmmmm – claims he must've lost that old knife of Alamo's when he fought with Waco. Says Waco musta picked it up – fact, he and Lucky rode back to look for it but it'd gone by then – so had Waco...'

'Listen, Marsh, I never saw no knife!' Waco said, emphatically denying the implication. 'Only when me and Lucas ran into

177

the ranch office and found Morg dead – the knife was lyin' beside him. *That's* where Blaine dropped it!'

'Well, I guess it'd make sense that way,' the lawman admitted. 'Now, scatter, do your best, and meet up at Fool's Canyon by sundown.'

Lucas made sure Waco was with him and Lucky Kinnane and Calico tagged along but Lucas got rid of them quickly enough, despatching them to check out dry gulches more to the north.

'You think Kilgour's on Blaine's side?' Waco asked worriedly.

'If he was stone cold sober I'd say "no" – but he's half drunk already an' he could let his personal feelin's override his Lawman's sense of duty...'

'Well, what we gonna do?'

'Stick to our story – we left Morg and Blaine alone, heard Morg shouting and soon after there was the gunfire. We ran back, found Morg dead – and saw Blaine lightin'-out towards town. We don't change that for anything! Marsh'll have to believe us then... We're lucky, it looks bad, Blaine leavin' the trail crew in town, then sending the rest of the hands in for a booze-up. Like he *wanted* to get Morg alone.'

Waco was willing to go along: he knew he could prise a lot more than two hundred bucks out of Lucas now. If Lucas could get rid of Blaine he'd have the ranch all to himself. And as Waco had opened the door for him to claim Broken Wheel, surely he would be justly rewarded.

These were the thoughts he had as he crossed a creek on the south side of the river. Then suddenly something hissed and he started to turn his head. Next instant he was gasping for breath, clawing at his throat and some unseen force dragged him violently from his saddle...

Lucas, expecting to meet Waco by the big beech just opposite the smaller set of rapids in the creek, wondered what was keeping the man. He started cussing Waco in his mind and then the brush behind him rustled gently, although there was no breeze at all, and his head seemed to explode like a firework going off behind his eyes...

Both men came round at about the same time. Waco rubbed at his throat and the raw rope welt that encircled his neck. The back of his head throbbed, too, where he had landed on it after being dragged out of his saddle. Lucas felt sick and his eyes seemed crossed, everything he looked at appearing double and blurred. He retched painfully.

'Take your time.'

They snapped their heads up at the quiet voice, and immediately regretted the unwise motion.

They saw Blaine, sitting on a rock by a small fire in a trench with a line of rocks around the edges, effectively shielding any glow.

'I've just finished my supper – left a little coffee warming on a nice set of coals, *hot* coals – you fellers interested?'

'The posse'll nail you before morning, Blaine!' grated Lucas, still feeling sick.

'They do, you won't know anything about it, Lucas – how about you, Waco? You want to gamble on the posse getting here in time?'

Waco swallowed – it hurt his throat. 'In time for – what?'

'To save you.'

Both men stared.

Lucas stammered, 'S-save us? From – what?'

'Me.'

Lucas felt his eyes widen and his mouth was suddenly very dry. He couldn't force out any words.

Waco frowned and his harsh voice was taut with concern as he said, 'You ain't gonna do anythin' with the posse so close!'

'How close you reckon they are?' Neither man hazarded a guess and Blaine said, 'They're way over in Fool's Canyon wondering where you are – miles from here.'

'W-what d'you want?'

Blaine swivelled his one eye to Lucas. 'Give it some thought. No hurry.'

Waco scowled. 'Gimme my gun and I'll...'

'You'll die, Waco – I'll put a bullet in you the moment you try for your gun. Mightn't kill you then, but you'll die eventually.'

Lucas felt really sick now. After Alamo and Blaine had gone to Mexico, Clay Winton had found some human remains half-unearthed by coyotes back in the hills where some rocks were splashed with what looked like blood. The dogs hadn't left much but had apparently been disturbed before they had finished their gruesome feast. There was enough left to see how horribly the men had died: they had been scalped, mutilated. There was a battered religious medal in the pocket of one corpse's shirt, one that Clay knew had been carried by Clem Hardesty – no churchgoer, but a man who cared for his mother who had given him the medal on her death bed.

Although it had never been proved and no one had asked Blaine, it was generally accepted that the remains were those of Hardesty and Clint Rendell, that Blaine had caught up with them, taken his revenge and buried the bodies before Alamo had whisked him away to Mexico.

Lucas somehow now knew for sure that Blaine had tortured these men who had caused him to lose an eye and almost his life. He began to shake uncontrollably. Blaine glanced at him, turned his attention back to Waco.

'Which one of you shot Morg?' No reply, of course. Blaine pointed at Waco. 'I favour you, Waco – you're the hothead... You all figured I hated Morgan O'Day and one day planned to destroy him. Nope – can't say I liked the man much, for he really wasn't much of a man. But he gave me a life even if he hated doing it, and he kept his word to my mother – I figured I owed him and I aimed to pay him back all the money he'd spent raising me. Then I aimed to move on and make a life of my own. He could've shot me but I wouldn't have drawn against him or shot back... And I sure wouldn't've put three bullets into his back and then run for it and thrown only the second real drunk in my entire life...'

'You can't prove nothin'!' Waco said. 'That knife's the clincher – most of the Broken Wheel crew knew you'd kept it from Alamo's things – you're the one gonna hang, breed! You got no chance with a white jury.'

Blaine stood slowly, stretching a little. 'You could be right, Waco– So I don't aim to take my chances.' He went to his saddle leaning against the rock and took his lariat, shaking out a loop. 'I reckon that cotton-wood just across the fire ought to be good, Waco – branch is just high enough for your feet to clear the ground.'

'Christ!' breathed Lucas in horror. 'You – you're not gonna hang him – *now!*'

Blaine said nothing, shook out his loop and turned to Waco. The man was breathing hard through distended nostrils, crouching – and then suddenly he was launching himself in a headlong dive for a smaller rock where Blaine had piled Waco's and Lucas' guns.

Blaine tossed his loop and it settled over Waco's head and the man twisted violently sideways, getting one arm through the rope so it couldn't tighten on his neck. But Blaine yanked hard and pulled the man back in a violent move that brought Waco almost upright and then he fell backwards.

But he had managed to snatch his Colt and he fired wildly and then Blaine put tension on the rope again. And for the first time, Waco realised they were on the side of a steep slope. As he brought the Colt around again, shooting, Blaine hitched the rope up over his shoulder and started to run down the dark slope. Waco was snapped off his feet and he yelled as he crashed face down on the stony ground.

Blaine's leg muscles strained and his teeth bared with effort as he lunged down the slope at reckless speed, hauling the wildly twisting and somersaulting Waco after him. The man hit his head on a rock, smashed a collar bone against another, screamed long and loud as the sharp gravel tore and shredded his clothes, then did the same to his flesh. He had still managed to hold on to the gun but was sobbing in pain and fear now as Blaine plunged into the creek shallows, spun, and his hands on the rope worked in a blur as he dragged Waco the last few yards over broken rock.

The man lay there, slobbering, snorting, gagging, a bloody mess, little better off than if he had been dragged by a horse. But he managed to focus on Blaine as the man waded ashore and with a roar, driven by pure hatred, he reared to his knees, clasped his Colt bloody handed and fired.

Blaine staggered, drawing and shooting instinctively.

Two bullets ended Waco's misery and the man sagged slowly, fell over the edge of the bank with his torn face submerged in the muddy waters. Blaine held a hand to his right side, awkwardly waded ashore, tangled his legs in the floating rope. He floundered – and it saved his life.

Lucas came skidding down the hill, with the butt of a rifle braced into his hip, and blazed at least four shots. They zipped into the water and passed over Blaine's head as he twisted on to his wounded side, actually afloat in the water. His gun hand broke through the surface, trailing silver.

He triggered, saw Lucas' right leg kick out from under him and the man fall. Blaine waited until he had stopped sliding and was beginning to sit up. Then he fired again and Lucas slammed over on his back. Blaine dragged himself out on to the bank, breathing hard, feeling the hot pain starting in his right side now. He pulled himself up and crawled to where Lucas lay.

He was sitting beside the man, right hand on Lucas' bloody chest, when Marsh Kilgour and his men rode in.

Blaine looked up with gaunt, wolfish face. 'He's still alive – ought to last long enough to tell you what really happened with Morg...'

*Or*, Blaine thought to himself as Lucky and Calico came running down the slope towards him, *Lucas might still have the last laugh and tell the sheriff and everyone else who could hear that Morg's death had happened just the way he'd told it...*

And that's what Lucas did. Then, as the life-light faded from his eyes, he gave Blaine one last twisted smile, gasping,

'G-get outta – this one – if you can, you lousy – breed!'

It was enough to make Marsh Kilgour frown thoughtfully but he still arrested Blaine after having his wound attended to and locked him up in his jail to await trial...

A man Blaine knew was named Calvin Eastbrook and who handled Morgan's legal affairs, came to see him three days before the trial was to begin.

'I have in my possession a letter from Morgan O'Day marked "To Be Opened Immediately Upon My Death" – I opened this, of course, as soon as I heard about his murder a couple of weeks ago. There was another letter inside to be mailed to his daughter, Kitty, who apparently is staying or working at some kind of Mission near Monterrey. He professed to disown her, but I know from his Will that this was only an outward appearance. Privately, Morgan was very concerned for her welfare and, I suspect, loved her as much as he ever did. He was really a lot softer than he allowed the world to see.'

Blaine made no comment although the lawyer waited, clearly expecting one.

'Well, to cut it short, he left Kitty a quite large sum of money to be used as she sees fit.' Eastbrook, a dour man with a thin moustache that had waxed ends, looked steadily at the wounded man. 'He left half of Broken Wheel to Lucas, if he still lived at the time of Morgan's death – if not it went to Kitty – and the other half was to be sold off – except for Fool's Canyon and six hundred acres surrounding it, including that coat-hanger bend of the big river. That, my friend, was to be your legacy – providing, also, that you were still alive at the time of Morgan's death – perhaps you'd care to comment now?'

Blaine, his face blank, said, 'I can't believe he thought that much of me.'

The lawyer snorted. 'You were too busy

being the injured party, the half-breed no one fully accepted, with a chip on your shoulder – you probably didn't notice yourself what was going on around you – Morgan was a man who spoke his mind, often in haste. The number of times I've had to change his Will, then change it *back* again simply because in a fit of pique he cut this beneficiary or that out, or gave them more, then changed his mind–' He sighed and shook his head. 'You confused him, Blaine: he hated the half of you that was Yellow Wolf, the man who destroyed his Katy, but he cared about *her* blood that still flowed in your veins. I believe his Will shows the truth of that.'

Blaine shook his head slowly. 'This has really floored me, counsellor – but it's not going to do me much good, is it? Marsh Kilgour's already contracted with Benny Calhoun and his sons to build the gallows.'

'Linus tell you that?' As Blaine nodded, Eastbrook almost smiled. 'He just wanted to give you something to worry about. Oh, I'm not saying the gallows will not yet be needed but no such contracts have been signed or even offered – in any case, I don't think you have to worry.'

'Why's that? Lucas made his death-bed

statement that I murdered Morg. A dozen men heard him...'

'Ah, yes, but Marsh Kilgour is not as weary or as dull as some folk think – just because he's old and ailing. He still is a lawman through-and-through and he's made his investigation and he's convinced that there is considerable doubt as to the veracity of Lucas' dying statement, or even the lucidity of Lucas' mind at the time he made it...'

'Don't give me any false hopes, counsellor,' Blaine told the lawyer quietly.

'That is not my intention. In any case, Miss Kitty O'Day, hearing about your predicament – I took the liberty of making her aware of this – has engaged me to defend you, entirely at her expense, of course– I have a very efficient investigative team, Blaine, and I assure you that when we go into that Court Room, we will do so quite confidently...'

'You'll hurt your arm, patting yourself on the back like that, Eastbrook,' Blaine said, but he felt giddy with the news the lawyer had given him.

*Kitty still cared for him! She had hired this smug lawyer to defend him – surely that meant something, something – special!*

189

'Like that feeling I had down at the Mission,' he murmured, unaware that his words could be heard by Eastbrook. 'I *knew* we'd be together again some day – with a little luck...'

Calvin Eastbrook's waxed moustache twitched at the ends – whatever that meant – and he said, 'Luck does not enter into it, Blaine– Be assured that Miss Kitty has hired the best defence lawyer in the land to act for you – the *very* best!'

Blaine lifted his head and stared at the lawyer.

Eastbrook arched his eyebrows, began to gather his things, preparing to leave.

'By the way, she'll be arriving here on the morning's stage...'

Blaine continued to stare, said nothing.

But he was thinking plenty.

The publishers hope that this book has given you enjoyable reading. Large Print Books are especially designed to be as easy to see and hold as possible. If you wish a complete list of our books please ask at your local library or write directly to:

**Dales Large Print Books**
Magna House, Long Preston,
Skipton, North Yorkshire.
BD23 4ND

This Large Print Book, for people
who cannot read normal print,
is published under the auspices of

**THE ULVERSCROFT FOUNDATION**

... we hope you have enjoyed this book.
Please think for a moment about those
who have worse eyesight than you ...
and are unable to even read or enjoy
Large Print without great difficulty.

You can help them by sending a
donation, large or small, to:

**The Ulverscroft Foundation,
1, The Green, Bradgate Road,
Anstey, Leicestershire, LE7 7FU,
England.**
or request a copy of our brochure for
more details.

The Foundation will use all donations
to assist those people who are visually
impaired and need special attention
with medical research, diagnosis
and treatment.

Thank you very much for your help.